LESSONS IN MERCY

LESSONS IN
MERCY

EDWINA WRIGHT DAVIS

This book is printed in the United States of America.

All scripture references taken from the King James Version of the Bible.

This book is a work of fiction inspired by the life of Joseph Daniel Herring. Some details from this story were obtained by personal interviews, newspaper and magazine articles and other archival resources. Permission to write the story was granted by the late Mr. Herring's wife. Some details and identifying names have been changed to protect the privacy of individuals.

Published by InSCRIBEd Inspiration, LLC. Roswell, GA.

Cover Design: Soleil Branding Essentials
Illustration: Lester Millsaps
Author Photo: Darren Freeman

ISBN 13: 978-0-9792385-9-8
ISBN 10: 0-9792385-9-5

DEDICATION

To Jefferson Herring whose love of family and family history has shed so much light on this book.

To Richard Herring, your photogenic memory of your family and dedication to history have made it a work of love.

This is for Dorothy Herring whose loving memories of her husband made this book possible.

CONTENTS

iii

AUTHOR'S REFLECTION

My name is Edwina Wright Davis. While attending an event at my alma mater in 2016, I was reunited with my friend Dorothy. As we sat in the auditorium of Bennett College, we chatted fondly about the twenty years we had not seen one another. The conversation led to updates about our individual families, our spiritual lives, and our dreams and goals.

I shared with Dot, "God told me He has chosen me to write the stories of His people. He has chosen me to write about unique assignments and miracles manifested through the lives of His chosen anointed."

Dot looked me squarely in the eyes and said, "Edwina, you ought to write about Joe." Dot's words were a confirmation for me. Joseph "Joe" Daniel Herring was Dot's husband of 45 years. I knew him personally and I had heard his story of redemption and mercy. Joe took the difficult lessons God taught him and used them as teaching tools. His story was one of God's unique consideration. Dot's words were a confirmation of my assignment.

Over a three year period I studied Joe's life with interviews with some of his beloved family members and close friends. By getting to know people who knew Joe, I saw the hand of God on every one of his experiences. I spent time with people he loved, shared his heart, and entrusted his personal legacy. My research methods also included searches of archives and newspaper clippings.

I recognized a pattern in the way Joe reacted to life's circumstances. In this fictionalized account, I want you as the reader to hear his booming voice and feel his caring persona.

In the black community, adoption, death in childbirth, infidelity, and physical or sexual abuses are often kept private. By the same token, human trafficking, race relations and class systems are not discussed openly. These are, however, predictors of behavior patterns and personal beliefs.

Joe's story includes these themes. The conversations that Joe needed most in order to understand and relate to his purpose were those things that his family did not talk about. For some, the subject matter contained throughout this book may be a trigger. I have chosen to include them with hopes that an open dialogue will bring individual and community healing. I hope you will glean lessons in mercy from Joe's life including the real meaning of family, faith in God, perseverance and the importance of not giving up.

Edwina

*"One generation passeth away,
and another generation cometh:
but the earth abideth for ever."*
Ecclesiastes 1:4

Flashing red and blue lights pierce the night sky. Three hearses nearly collide as they race to claim a dead body. Honking horns, screeching tires and blaring sirens rudely interrupt the quiet night as a fire truck and several police cars escort an emergency vehicle toward the hospital emergency entrance. A few yards away, flashing white lights indicate the entrance to the morgue.

In the meantime, three floors above the chaos below, in the neo-natal unit, a newborn baby cries.

This is the circle of life.

***

LESSONS IN MERCY

PART I: MY BEGINNING

My Birth Day

*"I never met a Herring
who was not proud to be one!"*
~Joseph Daniel Herring

I am told that April 7, 1928 was a brisk and overcast Saturday. Inside the small, well-kept house at 502 South Benbow Road in Greensboro, NC, an unpredicted and heartbreaking chain of events was about to unravel at the Herrings' home. The heartache and devastation that would follow would rattle the little house and the family inside to the very core! Nothing for us would ever be the same again! That tiny house on Benbow Road was transformed into a supernatural place.

Although my siblings were too young to understand anything about childbirth or even, as people say, "getting a new little brother or sister," they were smart enough to sense that something was going on. I am sure my family anticipated loving me as much as any of those who had preceded me.

3

I was not really Hanson and Eugenia Herring's seventh child. To put it more accurately, I was the seventh to survive. Two babies between Bertha Mae and me had died. Nobody expected my arrival to be any different than the others. There was no occasion for any fanfare or hoopla.

When all of this was taking place, my oldest sister, Bertha Mae, was weeks away from her fifteenth birthday. My brother, Elijah Hansen, was eleven; Nathaniel Graham, eight; Mildred, seven; Lizzie Ruth, five; and Ray, two. When I entered the Herring lineup that Saturday morning, the process was expected to be uneventful. The only unknown would be whether I would be a bouncing boy or a gorgeous girl.

Six little heads bobbed up and down and peeked from beneath the table and around corners. Six sets of eyes widened with curiosity, and six hearts beat rapidly as little feet scampered wildly around the room in search of a place to hide.

One child cried out, "Mommy, Mommy, where are you? Mommy?"

When she did not respond shrieks of fear came from the little ones. Another little voice was heard saying, "What's the matter with Mommy?"

Bertha Mae and Elijah were reassuring. They tried to quiet the tribe, "Shh, Mommy is fine." While this was obviously not a new experience for Pa, he paced nervously back and forth, in and out of the three-room house. I can imagine he was probably feeling cramped by the tiny space, six noisy youngins, a wife in labor, and a bossy mid-wife.

Although there was no fire, Pa brought in several armloads of firewood and piled them in front of the fireplace. There was fire on the stove and a pot of water boiling rapidly on top. About half a pan of biscuits that were left over from the night before sat on top of the stove along with fried white potatoes and several pieces of fatback.

Daddy returned intermittently and barked out a few commands. "Bertha Mae, heat up them biscuits. Put some butter and jelly on them and give them to your sisters and brothers, along with a cup of sweet milk. 'Ya hear me?"

"Yessir." Bertha Mae immediately complied with her instructions.

He called for my brother, "Elijah! Come out here with me and get up these sticks." He thought for a minute before he spoke, "Who put sticks all over the front yard anyway? You hear me talking to you? You can move faster than that."

"Yessir, Pa, I'm coming."

I Wore the Names…

The commotion that had begun much earlier in the morning reached a climax sometime before noon. The highly charged atmosphere of squeaks, squeals, moans, groans and other indescribable sounds, all at a deafening decibel level were suddenly, and eerily silenced.

Beneath the covers on the bed, my mother's legs and arms were flailing and flopping. I felt something warm, wet and sticky all over me, then I heard gurgling and gagging. There was a "White" woman, who just minutes before had been a "Black" woman, in the bed on all fours.

She was pumping, beating my mother on the chest, slapping her on the face, saying, "Come on. Eugenia, you can do this! Don't leave me! Come on, one more push…come on…" Then, pushing hard on my mother's belly with one hand, she grabbed my head with her other hand. The lady smacked me on my butt, cut something off of me with a pair of scissors, wrapped me really tight in a white towel, and put me in a dresser drawer.

The woman who had been first Black, then White, was now Gray. In a blood curdling scream, she cried out to my Pa, "Mr. Herring! Mr. Herring! Hanson Herring get here! Get here now!"

In the same voice, she began barking orders to Bertha Mae and Elijah, "Get these babies and take 'em out of here! Take them outside into the yard, next door to the church — anywhere! Just get them out of here. They don't need to see ya' Mama like this!"

Pa burst through the door. "What's wrong? Did something go wrong?" I think he was about to turn White, too. "God, no! No!" He bellowed in a voice sounding like that of a dying calf, "Is she…?" Pa fell to his knees gripping the side of the bed, groping and clawing at the bed covers like a wild animal. There was wide-eyed shock, horror and disbelief! "God, no. No!"

In the early 1900s, it was not unusual for a colored woman to have many babies and to have them in rapid succession. Nor was it unusual for her to die during childbirth. The wise, older women would comment, "She had those babies too fast — never gave her body time to re-build." I survived the birth process, but sadly, my mother died giving life to me.

From my beginning, I wore the names that my parents chose for me. They named me JOSEPH DANIEL HERRING. JOSEPH means "patriarch, favored son, given by God." In the Bible, he was given a coat of many colors. My middle name DANIEL means "delivered by God and God gives me strength." Daniel was a Hebrew prophet; a wise judge. He was delivered from the lions' den.

How could I, Joseph Daniel Herring at less than 24 hours old, recall the details of my birth? I have no explanation. No idea! Studies of the neurological functions of the brain show that the earliest age that memory begins is around three years. And, yet, here they are. It must have been the anointing of the Holy Spirit on my life.

The Anointing

". . . thou anointed my head with oil . . ."
Psalm 23:5

Pa never said to me, "Boy, you killed your mama."
Nor did any of my siblings ever accuse me of turning them
into orphans. My oldest sister, Bertha Mae, took Mama's
death harder than anybody, but even she never accused me
of anything. I always believed that nobody in my family,
especially Bertha Mae, appreciated the switch-up. In fact,
nobody in the family ever talked about Mama. The best I
could figure, it was that Mama and I were never in the
family at the same time. First, Mama was there, and I was
not. When I appeared my Mama disappeared.

I had no idea how to bring Mama back or how to fix
the problem I had caused. I just sucked it up, reached down,
picked up the "monkey" and put him on my tiny back.
You see, I did not understand that Jesus Christ had
shoulders that were broader than mine, and that He was
there to help me carry this burden of guilt. Years would
pass before I understood the words, He spoke to me on the
day I was born from John 14:18:

"I will not leave you as an orphan . . .
I will come to you."

Probably the most vivid memory I have of the day
of my birth was the big, black bus with "Brown's" written
in gold letters on its sides. This is an image that haunted me
for the rest of my life. Brown's Funeral Home was located
on East Market Street, around the corner and a few blocks
west of our house on Benbow Road.

Inside the house there was a bustle of activity as people bumped into one another. I could hear voices in the distance and vaguely discerned figures and faces. There was movement as people shuffled around. As my tiny body lay swaddled in that towel in the bottom drawer, I could see and hear everything, but I was not privy to anything. I saw people and furniture floating in the air.

I wanted to ask questions, make suggestions, talk about what was going on, but nobody listened to me. Everybody was totally oblivious to me. Even if they were paying attention to me, what could I say? I was a baby and wouldn't utter my first real syllable for over a year. The idea that I could communicate in any understandable way was laughable. But yet I understood exactly what was going on that day.

A wonderful Spirit entered the room when I was in the dresser drawer. He calmed the chaos, dismissed everybody else and spoke only to me. I still remember the sound of the Holy Spirit's voice and the words He said to me: "Joseph, I have chosen you. I will anoint you. I have a plan for your life. While you are still brand new, unspoiled and unbiased, I will begin to mold and position you for My plan." I felt a slight burn as the words of Jeremiah 29:11 were etched upon my heart:

> *For I know the thoughts I think toward you, saith the Lord. Thoughts of peace, and not of evil, to give you an expected end.*
> *Jeremiah 29:11*

From that day forward, this *Anointing* would enable me to discern what others could not see, hear what others could not hear, and prophesy future events. It would allow me to walk supernaturally in the midst of dark situations like Daniel did in the den of lions. It would give me comfort in difficult days; strength in my times of weakness and guidance and encouragement in times of conflict and confusion. While all of this sounded great, it was more than my newborn brain could comprehend.

I had many more questions than answers. For example: "What is an *Anointing*? What does it do for me? How does God choose whom He will anoint and whom He will leave alone?

The Holy Spirit never answered my questions. Maybe it was so loud he could not hear me. He just continued speaking to me in a calm, reassuring voice, "More often than not, you won't understand where I am going with your life. Frequently, things will get crazy, unfair and unfathomable, but hold on. I am equipping you with everything you will ever need to serve my purposes.

Still hovering over my cradle, or shall I say, my drawer, the Holy Spirit rocked me, gently and continued. "At times like these you must remember you have an anointing. Remember, I am your strength and you can call on Me. You will find that reminder in Deuteronomy 31:6.

"I guess that was my first out-of-body experience. At significant intervals throughout my life there would be others."

The sarcasm and quick-wittedness that characterized me throughout my life apparently kicked in at my birth. While the *Anointing* spoke to me, I asked a few questions of my own. "I am a newborn. I can neither talk nor walk. So how is it that you are giving me a purpose?

What is a purpose, anyway and what am I supposed to do with it?"

When the Holy Spirit mentioned that my life would sometimes seem "unfathomable, unfair and crazy," I had my comeback ready. "You don't say! What do you mean, …things will get crazy? Things are already crazy! Look at me stuffed in this drawer, and, by the way, would you pass me a towel, please?"

The Holy Spirit spoke clearly to me, "While you are still brand new, unspoiled and unbiased, I will begin to mold and prepare you for My intended purposes."

"What purposes? I'm a baby. Can I learn to walk first before you start giving out purposes?"

"You will not always understand where I am going with your life, Joseph."

"You don't say?"

"I am equipping you with everything you will ever need to serve my purposes."

> *"Trust in the Lord with all thine heart, lean not to thine own understanding.*
> *In all they ways acknowledge Him, and He shall direct thy paths. Be not wise in thine own eyes: fear the Lord and depart from evil."*
> *Proverbs 3:5-7*

I am glad that *the Holy Spirit* kept His promise to "…never leave or forsake me." Had He left me at any time, I would probably not be here, sharing my story with you today. I know now that what transpired on the day I was born was orchestrated and intentional. It was God's master plan for my life, one which would methodically unfold over the next sixty-six years, eight months and twenty-eight days.

From that day, The Anointing took control of my life. That's not to say that I did not fight in many situations. There were times when I wrestled with Him, went kicking and screaming, was bull-headed, and determined to do it my way. Truthfully, it was not always easy. It felt like having a younger sister or brother always on my heels, asking "where are you going? What are you doing? Why are you doing that?"

"...and one more thing, Joseph," the *Holy Spirit* interjected into my thoughts, "Since you asked, I will reveal your purpose. I have created you to be a teacher and an encourager. I will empower you with everything you need. Now go and walk into your destiny."

Even as early as day one, I liked having the last word, "Walk? ... really?"

"Every lesson you teach will come not from your lips, nor from your head, but from your experiences. Encouragement will come from the pit of your soul. Your students will look up to you, learn from you and respect you. They will all call you 'Papa'."

I wish I could tell you that this anointing made me perfect and my life easy. The truth is I got out of line or off track just like the next person. When that would happen, I felt a slight jolt as if I had been shocked by electricity. I called these my "and *then the light came on" moments*. The Holy Spirit would nudge me softly to be still and listen. The jolt would remind me of my action. When I did not obey, chaos and calamity were sure to follow.

> *"I called these my ...and the light came on moments, when the Holy Spirit would nudge me softly to be still and listen."*

The tragedy of my birth was actually not a tragedy at all. My life had purpose to glorify God. After years of wrestling I stopped messing up that part. My experiences became my teaching tools. These would be rich, colorful and sometimes brutal. Yet not one would come without a purpose or a lesson.

Growing Up a Herring and a Carroll

"Home is the place where
whenever you go they have got to let you in."
~Bill Cosby

Despite the horror and devastation of that fateful Saturday, life for the Herring family continued. We just needed time to establish a new normal. That's where family and friends came in.

Did Negro kids get officially adopted, or did some family member just take them in and raise them along with their own kids? In the days before adoption agencies, group homes and foster care, these types of social services were provided by family.

When a man lost his wife and was left with too many mouths to feed, a family member stepped in to lighten the load. Sometimes it would be a grandmother, a cousin, a church member, or a lady with no children of her own. My grandmother put it this way, "the person closest to the broom sweeps the floor."

Shortly after the news about my mama's passing spread through the family, my Cousin Sallie packed her suitcase. She traveled from the community of McDaniels and headed for Greensboro in Guilford County. Cousin Sallie was on a mission, "I am going to help my cousin by taking that baby off his hands."

I wondered for the rest of my life why my Pa, who already had six kids, would think of one more as that much of a burden. Who were these people, George and Sallie Carroll, that he gave me to?

I have already told you about my natural birth on April 7, in the little house on Benbow Road in Greensboro. If you go by the official U.S. Census records for the year

1930, I was born twice first in Guilford and then in Sampson County. Birth records in the Sampson county courthouse confirm everything I've told you.

According to the 1930 U.S. Census records in Sampson County, George Carroll 39, married 14-year old, Sallie (maiden name unknown). George was around 25 years her senior. By the time Sallie came to Greensboro to "take me off my daddy's hands," she was thirty George, was fifty-five. With me added, the Carroll family of McDaniels, NC, looked like this:

- George Carroll, head of household (55)
- Sallie Carroll (30)
- Louanna Crenshaw, adopted like me, niece (19)
- Sadie Carroll, biological daughter (15)
- Joseph Daniel Herring adopted son (2)

Growing up in the Carroll home on the east coast of North Carolina was great. The Carroll's included me in the family photos and referred to me as "our little Joey." I felt special as the only male child. Everybody loved me, and I had everything a kid could think of. McDaniels is a small, rural community adjacent to Elizabethtown. Actually, the two towns weren't even in the same county. Well-known Elizabethtown is in Bladen County, while the small, rural, mostly black McDaniels was in Sampson County.

Obviously, Elizabethtown, the "city," gave the area its reputation for being "bad and tough." That's where Negroes shot, stabbed or beat each other routinely. I grew up right in the heart of Bladen County. I guess you can't grow up in a place with a reputation for toughness without having some of that toughness rub off on you.

Mr. George was a big man with a hearty laugh, a bushy moustache, and a big belly. I can still remember him bouncing me on his knee, throwing me into the air, catching me, and tickling me until I couldn't stop squealing. I recall him perching me on his shoulders so I could reach the red cookie jar on top of the refrigerator.

Louanna and Sadie, were teenagers when I became part of the family. The girls must have loved the idea of having a baby brother because they loved playing with me and showing me off. They took me to school for *Show and Tell* and to Sunday School. They even spent their own money to buy baseball caps, nice clothes and toys for me.

George Carroll was a successful businessman. He owned a loading dock where large and small fishing boats brought fish to be sold. Mr. George and his twenty or more employees unloaded the boats, cleaned the fish, packaged them on ice and got them ready for resale to stores and restaurants, or individuals.

Mr. George owned Carroll's Great Seafood Restaurant. It was a big attraction to tourists and locals. Almost every Friday night, we would eat fish as a family.

Mama Sallie was a school teacher. She also was the Home Economics Agent for Bladen County. She visited high schools, churches and small groups, teaching Negro women how to become better homemakers. She taught them how to select the best cuts of meat and the freshest vegetables and fruits. She held classes on canning, preserving foods and gardening. Mr. George and Mama Sallie were an iconic pair.

Once they rounded out their family with me, we were a picture-perfect unit. My "parents" spent time teaching us about earning money, paying our tithes first, then saving and spending the rest. Nobody in George Carroll's household was afraid of work. We all held at least two jobs. By the time I graduated from Bladen County Training School for Coloreds, I had nearly a thousand dollars in a savings account at Waccamaw Bank.

As great as it was to be part of the Carroll family, there still seemed to be something missing in my life.

One Big Family

Although I was too young to connect the dots, I did notice a difference when I was around my paternal grandparents. They lived nearby on a huge 20-acre tract of rich farmland. With them I felt comfortable, like, *you're ok, this is where you belong.*

My Grandpa Hanson Herring was the fourth generation of Herrings to live on that plot of land that extended from Sampson into Bladen county. I remember hearing him grumble about having to pay taxes in both counties, "I don't get much service from either one." He was one of the most well-known Negro farmers in the area.

After his children grew up and left Down East, Grandpa continued to plant large tobacco, corn, soy bean, cotton and peanut crops. He raised hogs, cattle, horses and chickens. If you asked Grandpa Herring why he continued to work so hard, his answer was always the same, "People got to work and eat in order to live, don't they?"

Up until the day he died, Grandpa, along with Grandma Herring continued to farm their land; not so much for their own benefit, but to give work and purpose to others around them. In years when the crops did not pay what they should have, Grandpa was said to have "gone into his personal stash" and paid the helpers a full salary. Grandpa would say, "I believe everybody ought to feel that he's worth something to somebody."

> *"Grandpa would say, 'I believe everybody ought to feel that he's worth something to somebody'."*

He talked with young boys about values like finishing school, getting more education, taking care of their families, owning land and saving money. He cautioned them, "Don't throw your money away on

19

whiskey and wild women." I learned a valuable lesson about what it means to be family with shared values from him! Years later, I would find myself repeating Grandpa's exact words.

Although my grandparents stayed busy farming and mentoring, they did not neglect me, their own flesh and blood. My grandparents would often have Mama Sallie or Mr. George take me to their farm on Friday evenings. I would play with cousins or make a little piece of money picking crops from the garden or feeding the animals. Grandma taught me how to help in the yard and in the kitchen. Over the years, family members would accuse me of stealing Grandma's recipes for blackberry cobblers and homemade yeast rolls.

It was good to hear Grandpa and Grandma Herring brag to their friends that I was "Hanson, Jr's baby boy. He is smart as a whip!" It would have been even better to hear my Pa claim me as part of his family and to say he was proud of me.

Family Visits

A great cloud of dust would rise up from the long, dusty road that led from the highway, through the woods and down to Grandpa's big, white farmhouse. When the dust settled, the dogs would bark and you could see my Pa's maroon-colored station wagon with wood panels on either side. The car doors would fling open and all six kids plus Pa would jump out. At the same time the doors to the house would fling open.

Grandpa and Grandma Herring, along with any other relatives or friends who happened to be visiting, would run outside to welcome Hanson, Jr. and his kids from Greensboro. I lived for those family visits several times a year.

After an hour or so of bear hugging and backslapping, along with "look at how these kids have grown" and "get on in here and give me a hug," things would settle down. Depending on the time of arrival, there might be time for the men and boys to get some farm work done while the ladies started moving into the kitchen.

By the end of the day, there would be a mouthwatering meal prepared by the women in my family and a few other ladies from small neighboring farms. At times, there could be as many as twenty people sitting around the huge plank picnic tables in the backyard. We would enjoy navy beans, stewed tomatoes, green beans, fried chicken, and hot yeast rolls. There would always be homemade ice cream served on top of fresh fruit cobblers.

Mama Sallie would have started getting me ready for the visit a week or two in advance. "Joey, clean your room. Make sure you are caught up on your schoolwork and chores. Your Pa and the kids will be coming to spend some time with us. You can stay a couple of nights at

Grandpa Herring's. They have enough room for everybody to sleep in a separate bed and eat at the same table. After supper, you, Ray and Lizzie Ruth can come back here and sleep in this teepee I am going to set up for you on the screened-in back porch. How does that sound?"

"Whoopee!" I would exclaim.

"Will you kids be scared out there?"

"No Mama Sallie!"

"Mr. George will make a campfire in the backyard for you to roast marshmallows and chestnuts."

Ray, who is two years older, and Lizzie Ruth, who is four years older than me, were the greatest! Lizzie Ruth was a typical ten year old girl who liked bossing us around, "Joe, wipe your nose." She never kept anything from our dad, "Look, Pa, Ray is chewing with his mouth full."

Ray on the other hand, loved to tackle me, pin me to the floor and try to make me yell, "I give!" I was taller and almost as strong as he was.

Pa would schedule his trips to coincide with crop planting time in the spring and crop harvesting time in late summer and fall.

"Alright," Papa would say, "Ya'll, children behave yourselves. Do what your grandparents and Mama Sallie tell you to do, and no fussing and fighting. You hear me? I'll be back to get you before school opens. And remember you can keep the money your Grandpa pays you for working to buy school clothes, so don't throw it away on soda pops, candy, and trash!"

My Changing Life

Visits from my Greensboro family were routine until I reached age seven and the dynamics changed. By the time I turned seven, Bertha Mae was twenty-two and Elijah was eighteen. They were both out of high school and neither had any interest in working on a farm. They may have wanted to see their grandparents and little me, but it wasn't worth the trip.

Over the next few years, other siblings "aged-out" of trips down to the farm and eventually, nobody came to the farm or to see me.

By the time I turned ten years old, a lot of things in my life were changing. Louanna and Sadie had finished high school and moved away from home. One to attend business college and the other to get married. After that, I didn't see them anymore. Before the family dynamic shifted, I had already captured enough great memories to last me a lifetime.

I'm not sure what happened after my "big sisters" left home, except that things became a lot quieter. The atmosphere became somber. Mr. George stopped going with us to church on Sundays and had little to say around the house. I could not have a conversation with him anymore. If I walked into the room where he was watching television, he would get up and leave abruptly to walk outside or go to the bathroom.

Mr. George became evasive to Mama Sallie, who, although she tried to hide it, cried a lot. He didn't joke-around with Mama Sallie or smack her on her butt anymore. He didn't play with me or ride me into town on his truck either.

I guess things finally became unbearable between Mama Sallie and Mr. George right before I turned thirteen.

I returned home from school one day to find that Mr. George and all of his belongings were gone. We only used the living room for special occasions and Mama Sallie was crying softly as she sat on the sofa. I never heard his booming laugh or saw his face again. He disappeared from my life that day.

Some years later, I heard nasty rumors floating around town that Mr. George, experiencing male menopause and a midlife crisis, had fathered several babies. Allegedly including one with Louanna!

As I entered my teenage years, I began to feel a heaviness as if I were weighed down by something I could not talk about. I sensed a pattern emerging in my life. People who were supposed to love me and want me just kept dropping out of my life. I blamed myself, thinking I had done something to disappoint or run them away. Later, I flipped the script and began to see myself as the victim rather than the culprit. What had I done to make my Mama die…to make my Pa give me away…to make Mr. George and my half-sisters abandon me or my older siblings walk out on me?

Mama Sallie was the silver lining to the dark cloud that daunted my adolescent years. I know that she never got over the breakup of her marriage to Mr. George. He had been the love of her life. So even as she was going through her own hurt and embarrassment, she took time to understand what I was feeling. She always seemed to know exactly what was going on in my head and in my heart.

She was able to look beyond my faults and see what I needed. Mama Sallie never denied that I was fiercely competitive, angry and controlling. She knew that I always had to have the last word. This was long before the days of school counselors or family and child psychiatrists, but Mama Sallie in all her wisdom was intuitive enough to figure out that my behavior was connected to feelings of abandonment and rejection. How I felt was connected to my having been adopted and not kept with my family.

Mama Sallie spared no expenses to ensure that I got everything I needed to excel. She paid for tutors and for me to attend sports camps. Few, if any other Negro kids got this opportunity. She arranged for me to go with a select group of White kids to tour the state capitol in Raleigh and the Nation's capital in Washington D.C.

Because she was a teacher, Mama Sallie instilled in me a love for reading. She also made sure that I understood American History. Sometimes she would walk two blocks and do her grocery shopping while I read in the library. Other times, she would stay with me and read the newspapers and browse through her favorite cookbooks.

I must have devoured every book in the library. I read the World Book Encyclopedia by the time I graduated from High School. When the reading list for eighth graders was handed out, it included *Moby Dick*, *The Canterbury Tales* and *War and Peace*. I had already read them.

Because they wouldn't allow Negro children to check out books and take them home, Mama Sallie established her own routine for us. Starting from the time I was about four years old, she and I would go to the library and read for an hour every Saturday morning.

But in addition to these classics, I read every book I could find about a young, Negro baseball player from Cairo Georgia, by the name of Jackie Robinson. I was totally blown-away by this guy. I knew that I wanted to be just like him when I grew up. In my mind, I had a head start because I loved baseball, people said I "had a good arm" and I was a Negro!

Not only did Mama Sallie want me to read, she had me write a lot. The summer before my tenth grade year I wrote a letter to my Pa to ask if I could spend the summer in Greensboro with him and my younger brothers. By this time, he had gotten married two more times and had three more sons. Having somewhere to go during the summer was a big deal. A few weeks later he showed up on Mama Sallie's front porch.

Mama Sallie was letting me drive her car on the dirt roads because I had my learner's permit. As we pulled into the driveway after church, I don't know who was more shocked; me to see my Pa sitting on the porch, or him to see me driving a car!

Mama Sallie, Pa, and I went inside. I started to my room to change out of my Sunday clothes. I wanted to help Mama Sallie set the table and warm the pot roast we had cooked the night before. Mama Sallie shooed me away. "Why don't you turn on the tv and watch the baseball game? I know the Dodgers are playing. I believe Jackie Robinson is pitching. Go enjoy your Pa. I'll call you when dinner is ready."

About thirty minutes into the game, there was a knock on the front door. I opened it and there stood Grandpa and Grandma Herring. That was another pleasant surprise. Mama Sallie came out of the kitchen wiping her hands on her apron to give warm hugs and kisses to my grandparents. She invited Grandma into the kitchen where the two of them sipped tea, finished dinner, and waited patiently for the men to finish watching the game before they called us to the table.

My Grandpa sat on the left end of the sofa, chewing a wad of tobacco. My dad sat on the other end, puffing cigarettes. I sat between them, high on the feeling of belonging! I felt whole that day.

In the past, my dad had always wanted to get on the road to Greensboro before dark, but that evening was different. It was nine o'clock before anybody mentioned leaving. Grandma and Grandpa walked outside, first, followed by Mama Sallie. Pa followed his parents to their truck, hugged them tightly, and told them to drive carefully.

Next, he hugged Mama Sallie and told her how much he appreciated everything she was doing for me.

Finally, he grabbed me and gave me an awkward, bear hug followed by a slap on the back. At sixteen, I was already three inches taller than my Pa. His head rested squarely against my shoulder, and that's where I felt his warm tears. My knees wobbled a bit as I melted into his strong arms. After about thirty seconds, we moved apart. I mouthed the words, "I love you Pa." He got into his station wagon, turned on the ignition and drove away. I continued to stand there and wind-up my pitching arm when I noticed him coming back. When he got to where I was standing, he rolled down the window stuck his head out and said, "I got your letter, Son."

Shooting Pool

The best pool hall (actually the only one) in Elizabethtown was located at the bottom end of Main Street just before you crossed the railroad tracks into the Colored Section of town. Ham Fat's Pool Parlor was owned by a guy whose name was Forrest Parker. I don't know why everybody called him "Ham Fat," but they did. Despite the nickname, he wasn't even fat. He was a medium height, medium built redbone, and one of the nicest guys you would ever meet.

Ham Fat was not the stereotypical Redbone. He was taller, leaner, and had a lighter brown complexion than the average Lumbee Indian. Redbones were characterized by long, lean extremities and high cheek bones. Most had coal black hair that could be either straight or curly. Their complexion combined the smooth, black skin of Africans with the reddish -brown of Native Americans and the yellowish-white of White Europeans.

Ham Fat's people lived in nearby Lumberton, and more than likely, his mother, a pretty, young squaw had been taken advantage of by a dirty, old White man. His chiseled facial features, high cheek bones, pointed nose, and even white teeth made him quite handsome. I will tell you more about Redbones later.

From what I have observed in my daily life, they carried deep-seated resentment, bitterness and frustration. Some wore the scars of a people savagely mistreated and stripped of their significance. Ask Oprah's boyfriend Stedman about being a Redbone; he grew up in the area and could probably share a truth or two. Mama Sallie grew up in the community, had taught Ham Fat, and was well educated about the Native American tribes in the area.

Elizabethtown did not have much to offer colored kids in the way of recreation, so we had to make our own. Some of the boys my age enjoyed hunting deer, wild turkeys, wild hogs, rabbits, squirrels and all kinds of game with their Pas. A few kids liked fishing from the piers or deep-sea fishing from the boats. Perhaps if my Pa had lived close enough to teach me about these things and do them with me, I might have liked them, but he was in Greensboro with his other kids.

Grandpa Herring talked about taking me fishing and hunting, I don't know why, but he never did. That was okay with me, though because I found that what I loved more than anything, in addition to baseball, was playing a great round of pool. I got an adrenaline high from the sound of rolling balls and clacking sticks, hearing squeals of delight in victory and groans of agony in defeat.

Legally, I should not have been allowed inside the pool hall; I wasn't eighteen. I was only thirteen when I started hanging around Ham Fat's place, but my tall, muscular build made me look older. Ham Fat wasn't fooled by my size, but he allowed me to stay anyway. He knew that I was one of the many Colored boys growing up in a home without a father.

Ham Fat knew Mama Sallie and my paternal grandparents. He remembered that Mama Sallie was a Christian and a school teacher. She had taught him and had encouraged him when was growing up. He had probably grown up in the same situation, so he was noted for talking to us boys, giving us good advice and keeping us out of trouble. All the places taught the same lessons, but he just used a different language.

Ham Fat recognized that I was a good kid and that I wasn't going to do what I wasn't supposed to do, like trying to buy beer or cigarettes or betting money on the games. I knew better. There is no doubt in my mind that I learned as much about life from Ham Fat's Pool Parlor as I did from home, school or church.

Watching guys at the pool table was more exciting than any cowboy movie I ever saw. I also would rather spend a couple of hours in the pool hall any day than watch somebody score a touchdown or make a dunk. Pool was much more intriguing to me. I loved everything about the game of pool.

There was diversity in the pool hall, and it perpetuated its own culture. Men of all ages and all races came on payday for a much needed break. Some came after work, others who worked in the mills at night, came before work. Some came sober and left drunk. Others came drunk and left sober. Some left the same way they had come.

It was not unusual to find the basketball coach from the Colored high school playing against the White mill supervisor, while the preacher from the Black Baptist Church was looking on. On a Saturday afternoon, you might see the pastor circulating through the pool hall with a small soda and a hotdog in his hand as he spoke to the guys hunched over the tables. He would engage himself in their game and make small talk. Sometimes he would pick up the tab for their hotdogs and sodas but never for their beer or cigarettes.

The pastor would invite a man to church, "Come on out to church tomorrow. I see the wife and kids there most every Sunday." Amid head nods and balls clacking, "Be nice to see you sitting with them. I can't believe your boy has grown to be so tall and handsome." He'd take a sip of his soda, "What's he, about thirteen now? You know he plays the cello in the Youth Orchestra. I can only imagine what it would do for him to look out into the congregation and see you bursting with pride. It means an awful lot to a boy to feel that he has made his dad proud. Give it some thought. I hope to see you in the service tomorrow."

31

"Umm, Ok Rev," the man would respond nervously. It was awkward for everyone listening.

On any day of the week, except Sunday, patrons walked into an environment that was not only immaculate, but warm and inviting. Nobody was judged. Everybody felt appreciated and loved. I believe Ham Fat had a special gift from God that enabled him to see value in everybody. He even loved kids like me who weren't always loveable. For more than a decade Ham Fat never had any problems with me. "…and if I ever do," he would say matter-of-factly, "I know where you live."

All I wanted to do was hang out and watch the grownups. I could spend hours after school and all day on Saturdays racking balls, chalking sticks, and learning how to avoid a scratch. There was something about that highly charged atmosphere that made me never want to leave. I would help Ham Fat take black garbage bags full of beer cans and bottles to the dumpster, clean the bathrooms and sweep the floor.

On weekends and during the summer, he would let me stay late. Other times, he would say, "Ok Joey, go on home now. Help Mama Sallie with the chores and get your lesson. You can come back tomorrow." Occasionally he would go to his cash register, take out a couple of dollar bills and hand them to me. "Here. Ain't there a big football game at school this weekend? Cost to get in there don't it?"

"Wow! Thanks, Man."

"No problem, now get out of here."

***

The pool hall was a place where guys could swap lies about their women and about their winnings at pool and poker. They complained about backbreaking work on the pig farms, tobacco and cotton fields, and about long hours and low wages in the mills. As the evening wore on and the last beer kicked in, their moods changed.

What might have started as whining would eventually transform to anger and hostility. The men would get hostile and talk of double-crossing White folks, lying bosses, and job discrimination against minorities. Although I was just a kid, I realized that the men knew this cycle would never be broken for most of them. I vowed that when grew up and had my own family I would never live without a purpose.

At least, for the moment, they had found a place to enjoy themselves. These men could come to the pool hall, be loud and rowdy, sip a few cool ones, have a cigarette and curse a little. They ate pickled pig

> *"It had always been his dream to provide his community with a place of refuge from the storms of life."*

feet, beef jerky, pork rinds and hotdogs smothered with onions, chili and mustard. They would go home, only to return and repeat the cycle the next day.

Ham Fat's warm and outgoing personality and his cool calm demeanor made him a natural for the business. Ham Fat loved his work! You know what they say about that, "If you love what you do for a living, you can't call it work." It becomes your passion or your purpose. That is exactly what Ham Fat's Pool Parlor meant to Mr. Forrest Parker. It had always been his dream to provide his community with a place of refuge from the storms of life. He was living his purpose through the pool hall.

I Killed My Best Friend's Dream

There's a lesson here. Make sure you learn it. I had been out of high school for a few years and not doing too much with my life. I was hanging around Elizabethtown, but I would help Grandpa Herring on the farm when I could not avoid it. I worked part time in the mills in neighboring Roseboro if I had to make some money.

When I didn't have something better to do, I joined a couple of other dudes one afternoon and we stopped at Ham Fat's to shoot a few rounds of pool. I had not seen my friend in several months. When I walked in to the pool hall his face lit up like a Christmas tree. "Hey, Joey!" He grabbed me for a hug, "Man where you been? Good to see you Joey!"

I bear hugged him back. "Good to see you too, man. I've been working." My buddies and I found a table and shot several rounds of pool, between a few cool ones. The place had gotten crowded as my friends and I were preparing to leave. At one of the tables was a big commotion. Moving in the direction of the crowd, we found ourselves being shoved around. For a second, things went crazy in that place!

Ham Fat did not tolerate foul language or cursing God's name in his establishment. Hearing these young guys totally disrespect what Ham Fat's Pool Parlor stood for blew my mind. I started in their direction to tell them to cool it. The next thing I knew, some loud mouth, drunken kid was in my face saying crap that I wasn't going to take from anybody.

I let him have it. The full force of my iron fist landed right between the eyes! Blood went everywhere, and I heard the bone in his nose crunch. There was an explosion in my brain as I fell forward on top of the kid pinning him to the floor with my hands.

Amid loud shrieks of horror and people shouting at me, "Joe, stop! Stop it! What are you doing, you're going to kill that child!" The person inside my body kept banging the kid's head against the floor, choking, and punching him. It took four men to pull me off what turned out to be a tall, skinny kid celebrating his eighteenth birthday and having his first legal beer.

Sirens and flashing blue lights careened into the gravel parking lot filled with people, most of whom had fled the building when the ruckus started. The entire block was swarming with cops. Some cops dispersed the crowd outside and others came inside to handle the situation. Two cops easily identified me as the suspect because I was dripping with blood and sweat. They came over and fastened the iron bracelets around my wrists.

The police surveyed the damage I had done to the property. "This parlor looks like a disaster area," one of the cops sighed. "Check out all the broken pool tables, shattered glasses, broken light fixtures and broken chairs everywhere. This is a disaster zone."

As two rescue workers lifted the stretcher carrying the kid's limp body to the ambulance, another round of screams and moans erupted -- "God...who killed him?"

Someone shouted, "Is it Mozetta's boy? Oh Lord please don't let him be dead."
Once the pathway was cleared, the officers went over and talked with Ham Fat as they scribbled out a police report.

I was ashamed to look at Ham Fat, but as the officers were shoving me into the backseat of the police car, our eyes met. Although I would never see my friend again, the look in his eyes would stay with me.

Corner Pocket

"Great work, Joe!" I said to myself as I sat in the dingy four-by-four cell with a fragrance of urine.

I had been there more than twenty-four hours when a stern looking, red-faced police officer shoved a phone toward me through a tiny sliding glass window. "Judge just set your bail at $5,000. You need $500 to get out. You got three minutes for one phone call." He pointed to the glass, "Tap on this window when you're done. "

Another twenty-four hours passed before I heard footsteps again. I heard a key unlocking the rusty cell door. The same red-faced cop opened the door and motioned with his head for me to follow him. He led me down a narrow hallway and into a wide-open office. I took a deep breath for the first time. The office, unlike the place I had just left, smelled fresh and clean.

Mama Sallie and Grandpa Herring were already seated at a table across from a fiftyish, but not necessarily unkind looking woman. The cop directed me to have a seat in the empty chair. While the cop and the clerk were discussing some papers inside a folder Mama Sallie popped out of her chair and ran over to hug me.

"Everything is going to be alright, Son. I talked to the Lord all night long and then I got up, went down to the bank and got the money just like you told me. Your Grandpa was afraid that it might not be enough money, so he brought extra."

Grandpa Herring was a man of few words. As I slid into the chair between him and Mama Sallie, he clamped his big heavy weather-beaten hand down on top of mine and tried to console me. "Hold your head up, Boy. You ain't got nothin' to be ashamed of. You lost your temper and you done the wrong thing. At least ain't nobody dead.

Be thankful for that and let's move on. There's a lesson in this. Make sure you learn it."

The halfway friendly lady who was probably a mother herself handed me a form. "Sign this. You're more than eighteen, aren't you?"

"Yes mam. I'm twenty-two"

"Good, you can sign yourself out." I signed the paper and she said, "You are free to go."

Mama Sallie whispered loudly, "Give her the money. There's $500 in that little envelope from Waccamaw Bank."

"That won't be necessary." The lady behind the desk managed a compassionate smile. "My husband went to the hospital Saturday and spoke with both parties. The kid suffered a broken nose, collarbone, and jawbone and he may lose an eye. He lost all of his front teeth and had multiple facial lacerations, bruises all over his body, but he is alive."

> "Neither party wishes to press charges against you."

She took a deep breath and spoke again, "As for Mr. Forest Parker, I believe ya'll call him Ham Fat, he was hit in the face by pieces of flying glass. That's the physical part and that's not so bad, but emotionally, he's a basket case. They've got him on suicide watch over at the hospital; scared he'll try to hurt himself. He is inside a strait jacket and sitting with a vacant stare in his eyes. He can't even tell that his nose is running or that saliva is dripping from the corners of his mouth. He keeps blabbering, but the only words anybody could understand were, 'Tell Joey I forgive him'."

Mama Sallie began to sob. First, Grandpa Herring and then the White lady consoled her by putting their arms around her. After a while, Mama Sallie stopped crying and the lady was able to proceed. She slid two official documents across the desk in my direction. I looked at them through my own tears and saw that one had the kid's signature and the other had Ham Fat's. She read the questioning look on my face and said, "You don't owe us any money because of these two signed documents. Neither victim wishes to press charges against you. You signed the papers. You are free to go Mr. Herring."

Mama Sallie, Grandpa Herring, and I made one stop after leaving the jail. We went to Community Hospital, where the kid lay bandaged from head to toe. Sitting in a big chair beside the bed was a frail, scared looking lady in her mid-forties. When we entered the room, she jumped to her feet and rushed over to greet us. Recognizing us immediately, she spoke apologetically as if we were the victims rather than herself and her son.

"Doctor thinks he'll be well enough to get out of here, get back to school and graduate with his class. He had his heart set on going to college in the fall. He's been working and saving his money for college since he was about thirteen."

Mama Sallie wiped away the lady's tears and motioned for us to join hands in prayer. Grandpa Herring thanked God for forgiving hearts and for His mercy. He prayed for the kid's complete recovery. While our eyes were still closed and our heads were still bowed, Mama Sallie nudged me and said, "Go ahead, Son." I hesitated momentarily, then took the money which Mama Sallie had brought to the jail and handed it to the lady. "I am so sorry for what happened." I fought back tears, "Please forgive me for the pain and suffering I caused your family. Please use this money to help with his expenses."

She was surprised and grateful. "Thank you. Ya'll didn't have to come down here. I know this was an accident." She looked at me, "We ain't mad." She took the money from my hand, "This is a blessing."

Our next stop was on the seventh floor. We were not allowed to see Ham Fat. His wife came out to greet us in the waiting room. She was a beautiful, full-blooded Lumbee with a warm, friendly smile and coal-black hair that hung to her waist. Mama Sallie started to talk, but Mrs. Parker put her fingers to her lips and said, "No apologies needed. God knows your heart; you are already forgiven."

Nudging me again, Mama Sallie said, "Joey, go ahead and do what you came to do." I took the remaining cash from the bank envelope and pressed it into Mrs. Parker's hands. "Use this to help reopen the pool hall."

Pushing the folded bills back to me, she said, "No, Joey. That's not what Forest would want. He would want you to use this money to leave town. He would want you to make a better life for yourself someplace else." She looked me in the eye and spoke softly, "You know, Joey, you were always one of his favorites. He always said that you would do great things. If Forrest ever does come back to his right mind, yours will be the first name I will mention to him. I'll let him know that you have moved on to make us proud."

"Yes ma'am." It was all I could say. Every mistake comes with a lesson, I had to be sure to get the lesson in this experience.

And the Magic Began

I took the advice of my friend's wife. Less than a week after getting out of jail, I tearfully said good-bye to Mama Sallie, Grandma and Grandpa Herring, and other friends and family members. I packed up my earthly belongings and drove the seventy-five long miles to Roseboro, NC.

In no time, I got hired as a part-time worker in a local textile mill and rented a room from a nice family. One day later, I was learning my way around the town when I stumbled upon the Negro high school and noticed they were having a big event in the gymnasium. I decided to go since I had nothing else to do.

I walked into the building and saw a beautiful young lady sitting in the next-to-the-last unoccupied seat on the bleachers. As the shy looking girl leaned forward and looked down the row to hear the punchline of a joke somebody was telling, I saw somebody tug on her shoulder. "Hey, good looking, are you saving this seat for somebody?" Slightly startled, the pretty girl turned abruptly to find her space being invaded by a round, red, pimply face and a wide toothy grin. As she leaned backward to give herself a little breathing space and some time to concoct a polite refusal, the not-at-all cute guy repeated, "May I sit with you?"

She told me she sucked in a deep breath and told herself, "Think fast! Say no." Nothing came out when she tried to answer him.

Presuming a "yes," the big guy slung his book sack on the floor in front of the bleacher and started to lower his butt onto the seat.

I chuckled at her girlfriends further down the row who were no help at all! She opened her mouth and tried desperately to form a lie, "This seat is for my 100-year old mother, my blind brother, my crippled cousin..." but she wasn't making any sense. Her friends were laughing their heads off.

Time was running out and she had no idea what to do. Then suddenly she was saved. I was "Mr. Cool and Clean" from the big city of Elizabethtown who swooped down and swept cute, shy, and petite Dorothy Melvin off her feet! That's my story and I'm sticking to it. Dot's story may be different, so I'll let her tell her side.

Dot's Side

From out of nowhere, a second guy appeared and walked behind the fat guy. "Excuse me, Buddy, that's my seat. Would you get your stuff and move on down so that I can sit in it?"

I am sure that the "Chubby-Checker," look alike was dazzled trying to determine if this pushy person were the "old mother, blind brother or crippled cousin" but there was no time for him to figure it out. The lights were beginning to dim. The second voice gave a not so gentle push, "Come on, Buddy, get out of my seat. They are getting ready to shut down the lights."

With that, the guy stumbled blindly into the aisle to find another seat while "Mr. Muscular-tall-dark and handsome" slid easily onto the seat beside me.

The room was totally black, except for the stage. Our Principal stood in front of the podium holding the mic. "Today, we have a special guest for you. Mr. "Almost" Harry Houdini.

Not surprisingly, White kids and White schools always got the first and the best of everything in the South. Negro kids got whatever was left. When it came out in the local newspaper that some wealthy, White textile owner was bringing a distant cousin of the world's greatest magician to tiny Roseboro to entertain school kids, we paid no attention to it. We were sure that "local school kids" meant "local, white kids" only and we didn't care that much about magic. Give us baseball, football or basketball which was more our speed.

Our principal continued, "Let's hear it for Mr. Almost Harry Houdini." He led the audience in clapping. "Give it up for our guest." There was an uproarious round of applause and foot stomping against the wooden bleachers. As quickly as the clapping ended the principal's body was sliced in half. His head chest and torso fell to the floor and rolled in one direction while his legs, still clad in the blue and white seersucker pants galloped backward toward the curtain. The girls went wild trying to dodge splatters of blood splashed into the audience.

A weird looking creature with a sickening laugh romped onto the stage. Blood was dripping from the 5-foot-long machete he had used to slice our principal in half. I could not take it anymore. I screamed to the top of my lungs and covered my eyes. That's when the strong arms belonging to the stranger beside me slid around my shoulders and pulled me toward himself. He leaned over and whispered in his deep, reassuring voice, "Don't be scared. It's only magic."

Uncovering my eyes and turning to look at him, I was pleasantly surprised to see that he was handsome. "By the way, my name is Joe. Joseph Herring. What's yours?"

I could detect the smell of his cologne. It was the favorite and probably the only affordable cologne for guys back then. Minutes earlier, the roly-poly fellow had tried to talk to me, but no words would come out. The new guy and I just stared at each other for a second until the principal, his body back together, entered the stage blasting into the megaphone with a drumroll at his back, "Boys and girls of Roseboro High, "Sit back, relax, and let the magic begin!"

Husband and Wife

It must have been magic that made things move so quickly and smoothly with Dot and me. By the time she graduated from high school the following June we were going steady. By Christmas, we were married and making plans to leave tiny Roseboro. Both our hearts were turned to Greensboro. We were taking the first steps toward realizing our dream. You already know how, as a kid, I longed to live close to my dad and siblings. Dot, who had always loved figures, dreamed of going to A&T College and becoming a mathematician.

Although we were young, we were mature. I worked several jobs and Dot started her Freshman year in college. We were not afraid of hard work and we saved our money. We lived with my brother Wray and his family for the first year. They didn't charge us rent, but allowed us to help them with utility bills and groceries. Life was great for us!

Returning to Greensboro as an adult, after having grown up with my adopted family in McDaniels, was bittersweet. The relationship with my Pa and my siblings was a work in progress. We got to see him once or twice a week. I guess blood really is thicker than water. Dot and I worked to unify our family. We shared meals together and it seemed that Pa was excited about and loved playing with his grandchildren.

Passing Brown's Funeral Home still sent shivers through my body. Many years would pass before I would connect my jittery stomach and panic attacks to feeling guilty over my mother's death. In my head, my birth and my mother's death were inextricably bound. I could never think of one without thinking of the other. I could not love one without hating the other.

What a cruel trick for God to play on a kid! The same God who had promised at my birth, "I will not leave you or forsake you," is the one who took my mother from me!

> **What a cruel trick for God to play on a kid!**

Dot helped me understand a few things about my Pa. I had shared with her, shortly after we were married, the conversation I overheard between him and Mama Sallie. It had taken place on the front porch of Mama Sallie's house when I was fifteen years old. Dot reminded me, "Your Pa did what he thought was right by you at the time Joe."

I wanted to talk to my Pa about his decision to give me to Mama Sallie, but I never had the courage to bring up the subject. The closest he ever came to talking to me about it was to say, "Sometimes, son, men have to do what they think is best for their family even though it hurts." Dot had been right about him.

By the time we ended our first year of marriage, there were major changes in our circumstances. For starters, we had a beautiful baby girl. Nobody told us how hard it would be for Dot to care for an infant, be a full-time student and a wife. Unfortunately, even with that much amazing support, Dot could not withstand the pressure of her responsibilities. She flunked one of her major courses, combed out half of her big, pretty afro, lost weight and spent a lot of time crying. Although Dot's mother came from Roseboro, Mama Sallie came from Elizabethtown and Pa's third wife were there to help, Dot still struggled with her depression.

It broke my heart. I didn't know how to make things better. I did not realize it, but I had a lot to learn about my little lady from Roseboro. I didn't tell anyone, but I had picked up a haunting feeling that unless I kept her happy, Dot would leave me. That was not the case, she would be with me through much worse times.

46

The 1956 World Series

*"If there's a lesson in the loss you
ain't lost nothing."*
~Mary Hill

Shortly after Dot's bout with depression, Ray accepted a job as band director in a well-known Virginia high school. They allowed us to stay in their house, rent-free, until we found our own place. Ray told me, "I know you will take care of the house for me." I was glad to care for my brother's home.

Pa was a pillar for us. He offered money to help with bills and other necessities. Bertha Mae was especially supportive when Dot experienced her depression. She would come over to help Dot with the baby, prepare meals and keep her company. Although I still had nagging feelings about Bertha Mae's resentment toward me, Dot helped me see my sister's love for me and a light came on. Dot even said to me, "Bertha Mae and Lizzie Ruth feel more like sisters to me than my own sisters." I watched my sisters and Dot's mother nurse her back to health.

By the time Mrs. Melvin was ready to return home for the second time, Dot's health was much better. We had saved enough to put a down payment on our own house. We bought a brand new, three bedroom brick ranch with a deck on the back and a gorgeous yard.

Nothing gave me a greater sense of belonging than to pull under our carport and see my wife cooking dinner on the grill and our three kids: Pat, Lynda and little Joey playing. It was a pretty picture. My heart would leap with joy and tears of happiness would well up inside me. God gave me my very own family! Nothing on earth would ever tear us apart. I belonged to somebody and somebody really belonged to me!

What I liked most about our little house on Julian Street was that it was the hub of neighborhood activity. Kids rode bicycles and skated in the street. Wives left their doors open and went from house to house while we, guys washed our cars in the driveway. We fried fish, played cards and sat on our back stoops talking about religion, politics and sports.

Back in the fifties, radio was the center of home entertainment. I'd always followed the Dodgers, but until that year, I had only listened to them on the radio. I was twenty-eight years old and bursting with pride that I had saved $289.99 to buy my first television. It was a 17-inch Black and White Admiral that sat on a top of a big, mahogany table in our den.

I was proud that I could invite the boys who lived in my neighborhood to come and watch the Series with me. I knew them all; I knew they worked hard, but I also knew that they did not make enough money on their jobs to buy their own television sets.

In addition to working at Cone Mills and driving a taxi, I would cut up firewood with my chain saw and sell it to people in the wintertime. Not only that, when the city got ice and snow on its roads, I would go looking for folks that I could pull out of the ditches with my big truck and log chains. I did not quote a specific price for this job. I would just tell the people "Give me what you think it's worth." Most of them would gladly give me five or six dollars.

Every now and then, somebody would give me ten dollars. Sometimes a cheap dude would try to hand me a lone dollar bill. I would hand it right back to him and say, "You keep that, Buddy. I just did you a favor. May God bless you. Have yourself a good day."

I can still feel the tingle of excitement as Dot and the kids helped me put finishing touches on grilled hotdogs and hamburgers. When the guys in my neighborhood arrived to watch the 1956 World Series between Jackie Robinson's Brooklyn Dodgers and the New York Yankees.

The pendulum of social change was beginning to swing around that time. Throughout the United States, Negroes and White sympathizers were calling out racial injustice and demanding change. Even when my son Joey was in college, those protests and demands for justice were widespread. Jackie Robinson was at the center of change.

By the time the game started, there were eleven of us in my den, waiting for the action to begin. Pa was sitting comfortably in the plush, brown recliner that Dot and the kids had given me for my birthday. Seeing him in my chair looking like an older, shorter version of me made me happy. My brother, Wray, along with his brother-in-law, and six others were tuned in for the action. My buddy John Courts rounded out the gang. John enthusiastically led us in singing every baseball chant as we watched the game.

It was good, stiff competition. Everybody was betting on somebody. All the Negroes I knew were betting for the Dodgers, because for the first time in American baseball history, the team had a Negro player. For the same reason that all Negroes were pulling for the Dodgers, all the White folks were pulling against them.

On Wednesday, October 3, 1956 eyes and ears around the world were tuned into radios and televisions to watch the first game of the World Series. Ebbets Field was full of 35,000 screaming fans ready for the action.

All around the globe, fans gathered for the big game. They huddled around dilapidated picnic tables in muddy backyards in the South. They sat in smoke-filled, dimly lit pubs in Europe. They sat around tiny kitchen tables in the Midwest. In the North they sat on bleachers in vacant lots. Fans gathered wherever they could get their ears and eyes glued to portable radios and to electric television sets. The sound was uproarious as men shouted at each other and banged their beer bottles and fists on the tables. They slapped each other on the back in comradery. As long as they were sober enough to be coherent, everybody was shouting and chanting.

In the first game, the Dodgers beat the Yankees six to three. Jackie Robinson hit his first homerun for the series. Man, it was pretty! Jackie Robinson had hit a homerun to clench the win in game one. Life was good…and you couldn't tell a Negro nothing! Ha Ha Ha! Man, that was one of the best days of my life! Then Gil Hodges hit another one and that was all we needed to seal the coffin. There was no game on Thursday because of rain. But, on Friday, October 5th, it was game on.

Game #2 was a killer — what heart attacks are made of! 36,000 fans thundered as they watched! The game vacillated back and forth for nine breathtaking innings and the excitement never diminished. At the end of the first inning, the Yankees led 1 to nothing. Inning two ended in a tie -- six all! In innings three, four and five, the Dodgers forged ahead to an eleven to seven lead and never looked back. Amid deafening shouts and roars, they won thirteen to eight!

I felt pride in my people. I felt pride in myself because I had a good job, a good wife and kids and a nice home. The American dream seemed attainable. What a good time to be alive!

I bet my Pa twenty-five cents on game two. I had taken the Dodgers and gave him the Yankees. At first, he insisted, "I don't want to take your quarter son. But I will."

I was adamant. "Come on! Come on, Pa!" I was all in his face. He wasn't one to turn down a bet. "Let's see who wins Pa."

"Alright, Boy, put your money where your mouth is. And don't say nothin' when I put your puny, little old quarter in my overalls' pocket 'cause, when I win it, you ain't getting it back."

"Why has my quarter got to be puny, huh? A quarter is a quarter. Mine is as big as yours. Ain't it?" For good luck, I took my quarter out, smacked it on the back of my hand, then on my forehead and then on the table. Pa did the same with his.

I won my Pa's 25 cents! Man, did I like the feeling of winning a good bet! There is nothing like it! When Duke Snider hit that unforgettable homerun more than 400 feet down centerfield, I nearly jumped three feet off the floor. We already had the game in our hip pocket, but Snider's homerun made it sweeter. The Brooklyn Dodgers had won the first two games of the World Series.

As Pa slowly slid his quarter across the plank table toward me, he said, "Here Boy. It's yours. You won it fair and square. Now, you want to bet on the next game?"

Of course, I did.

We lost games three, four, and five. I was mad they had shut us out. We had to win games six and seven. It was just that simple. We couldn't let them damned Yankees win another baseball game.

Game time on October 9 was 1:00 PM at Ebbets Field. The Yankees led us in the Series by one game. We knew how to fix that. We could win game six and make it a tied-series. Then we would come back tomorrow and beat the snot out of them for a series-winning game seven.

History was in the making and game six was about to begin. In a 10-inning scoreless pitching duel with both starters going all the way, Jackie Robinson's walk-on single to left field in the bottom of the tenth inning won the game and kept the Dodgers' championship hope alive.

Wednesday, October 10, 1956, the series was tied, three and three. Everybody's jaws were jacking. Everybody's lips were flapping. "Come on, everybody. Put your money right here. Winners, split, losers, git!" Of

51

course, I was going to add to the pot. I took the quarter I had won from my Pa on game two, added three more to it, along with four folded $1 bills and slammed them into the pot with all my might. It was a sweet pot with nearly $50 swimming in it.

It was game seven, bottom of the ninth, when Jackie Robinson picked up his bat and strode to the plate. With every bit as much power, focus, and deliberation as he had shown in game one, he swung, and missed three times. That was a heartbreaker! My team, the Brooklyn Dodgers, lost the World Series to the New York Yankees in game seven. They killed us nine to nothing!

Grown men cried. As we picked up our proverbial crying towels and dabbed our eyes, we reminded each other, "Hell! We've been disappointed before; ain't nothing new about this. Negroes are always getting disappointed for one reason or another.

In the face of his loss, Jackie had just scored his biggest win. He had stayed true to himself and had not allowed anyone or any circumstance to define him; nor had he allowed racial bigotry or ignorance to reduce him to a lesser man.

Sacrifice Hits and Bunts

*"...Always a team player, he (Jackie Robinson) regularly
laid down bunts and sacrifice-hits to allow teammates
to advance and score."*
~Evan Andrews

Rudolph, Reggie and a few other republican
Negroes who were brazen enough to come to my house and
root for the Yankees were happy as punks in a penitentiary
when they won. The Son-of-a-guns high-fived each other,
did a happy dance, divvied up the "pot" and left grinning.

"We'll get them next year," I thought to myself as I
pushed through the storm door to our backyard. Raking the
last batch of hotdogs and hamburgers from the grill onto a
big platter, I took them inside and put them on the kitchen
counter. "Alright, boys, eat-up. I can't keep all this food for
my family."

Everybody grabbed a second, third or fourth hotdog
or burger, squirted it with condiments, then headed back to
my den. Shortly afterward, several other guys had to go
home. That left three of us to guzzle down the last of the
cold ones before settling back to analyze what had gone
wrong in game seven and to solve the world's problems.

John Courts was adamant, animated and jumping all
around when he talked about the loss." He could have
caught that one in game four!"

"Why didn't the dumb umpire call that strike in
game five?" Jim took a sip of his beer.

John beat his hand on the table, I laughed. "The
umpire called that ball in game five, but it should have been
a strike!"

I agreed, "A blind man could have seen that! I don't
know what was wrong with the umpire!"

"That third base coach had to be blind, crippled and crazy!" We all laughed at John when he spun around.

Gus, who was usually quiet spoke up, "Why did they put that clown up to bat anyway? He couldn't hit the broadside of a barn!"

John jumped again, "Rigged!! Oh, what the heck!" John exclaimed, "My paycheck will be the same, no matter who won."

"Damn!" I sighed, "Sure would have been nice to see Jackie win, though. Maybe next year!"

Pa chimed in, "Naw. Too soon for that. They weren't going to let a team with a Negro on it win the World Series, yet. White folks in America ain't ready."

I agreed with my Pa, "You are damn right. He was handpicked. What's wrong with that? They couldn't just put anybody out there to play." I turned to my friend, "Can you see them picking a Negro with as much mouth as you have John?"

"He was going to have to be a Colored boy with a strong arm, jack-rabbit legs, and a good head on his shoulders. He needed thick skin, a strong backbone and a tight lip."

I knew that Jackie Robinson had everything they were looking for. The newspapers said that Brooklyn Dodgers' General Manager Branch Rickey hand-picked Robinson to break down the racial barriers in a major American sport. As I see it, Rickey could not have made a better choice. Here was a kid born at the right time into a poor Negro family. He not only had a passion and a gift for baseball, but he had the attitude of a winner. That meant subjecting himself to rigorous training and staying focused on his goals despite the nasty distractions he encountered.

Robinson's journey was never easy. He faced racism from his own teammates as well as from players on opposing teams. Soon after his debut with the Brooklyn

Dodgers on April 15, 1947, some Dodgers players signed a petition to prevent him from joining the team.

Later, there was a newspaper article about one incident in Syracuse, NY, where a rival player threw a black cat onto the field and chided, "Hey, Jackie, there's your cousin." After hitting a double and later scoring, Robinson quipped about the incident, "I guess my cousin is pretty happy now."

It was not unusual for Robinson and his family to receive death threats. One such threat, before a Cincinnati Reds game, was so convincing that the Feds were called in to investigate the matter. A mysterious source calling itself "Three Travelers" sent letters to the police, the Reds and a local paper. They vowed to shoot Robinson with a scoped rifle as soon as he stepped onto the field. Robinson was not deterred. He played in the game and to fans' delight, belted one of his iconic home runs that day.

Robinson was known for his skill at bunting and being an electrifying base runner. Always a team player, he regularly laid down bunts and sacrificed hits to allow his teammates to score.

The Mill Culture

The Industrial Revolution, birth of modern industry, and the social changes that accompanied it started in Great Britain. By the 1800s, the revolution had found its way to the United States, and textile companies had built hundreds of mills to house the large machines used to weave and color fabrics.

In the Deep South, where cotton was king, the mills were a natural step in the progression of cotton from the fields to the fabric shops. In the mills, cotton was transformed from the boll into the bold and brilliant hues and designs of fabric. Not only was the process revolutionary, but the economic and social changes that came along with it were also revolutionary.

The click-click sounded non-stop for what seemed like forever. Actually it took only 90 seconds for fifty employees to punch the clock. At precisely 3:30 the time clock mounted on the concrete pillar in the back of the mill would allow the first third-shift worker to punch in. The smart system was designed to allow up to fifty employees to hit the clock within a three minute time frame.

Anyone punching in after 3:33 was late. More than three late punch-ins within a two-week pay period resulted in a fifteen-minute pay cut. No, you couldn't make up the late minutes by staying a minute longer at the end of the shift. The clock was too smart to allow that.

I spent a lot of time studying men and women as they filed into Cone Mills textile plant to begin their third shift tour of duty. I was struck and annoyed by some glaring discrepancies in demographics; the most obvious was race. I would say that out of 100 employees reporting for nightshift, maybe a dozen were White. They were quality control operators and supervisors walking around with clipboards in their hands and pencils behind their ears. White females were stenographers, typists, and clerks.

I suppose White entitlement perpetuated the myth that Negroes did not care about sitting down to eat together as a family or about supporting our kids at PTA or after-school activities. They must have believed we would work any hours and be happy. Those of us Negros who worked third shift did not have schedules that were conducive to family life.

The lower paying, backbreaking and environmentally hazardous jobs were left for us. As machine operators, we sat in straight back, metal chairs for four hours consecutively. We only had a five-minute break. The concrete floors offered little forgiveness to tired, aching legs and backs that pushed carts loaded with heavy bolts of fabric from one side of the plant to the other.

Other Negroes worked in the dye rooms, inhaling toxic fumes from the lead-based dyes. Chronic itching eyes, runny noses and dry, hacking coughs were hazards of the job. Nobody paid much attention to the large number of Negro mill workers who suffered, and even died, early from illnesses like emphysema, tuberculosis, Chronic Obstructive Pulmonary Disease (COPD), asthma and throat cancer. The Occupational Health and Safety (OSHA) agency and the Environmental Protection Agency (EPA) were nowhere to be seen during those times.

Last but not least, we were janitors. We cleaned the bathrooms and breakrooms, swept cigarette butts, and picked up trash in the parking lot. In the winter we cleared ice and snow from the docks and walkways. In the Spring and Summer, we mowed the grounds and raked leaves. Throughout the year, we collected trash and took it to the dumpsters at the back of the plant.

I could almost count ten Negro women to every Negro male. This troubled me for several reasons. Most of these women were married, had children, lived in government subsidized housing or the projects and went to church on Sundays. So where were their husbands working, if not at the mill? Who was supporting their children and who was paying the rent? Why did male mill workers own cars while the females relied on public transportation or taxi cabs to get to and from work? And, most troubling to me was if someone was home to monitor their kids after school or help them with homework?

As I viewed mill work especially for Negroes, it was a total distortion of what I believed male and female roles were supposed to look like. With bitterness and resentment, I blamed Cone Mills for hiring a Negro woman while refusing to hire her husband. It perpetuated in her a sense of dominance, while creating in her man inferiority and inadequacy. With equal passion, I resented the Negroes who bought into the labels that Cone Mills and the rest of White America placed on us.

I always seemed to have gut feelings about what was right and what was wrong. I believe that had something to do with my anointing by the Holy Spirit on the day I was born. Remember how He said that, "I would teach others?...that my own life experiences would be my teaching tools?"

The last thing I'm going to say about the inequity in the mill population is this: every Negro, with one exception had at least a high school diploma. Mr. Richard Black was the only one of us who did not have higher education. He started with Cone Mills as a janitor and errand boy when the first plant opened at the end of the 19th century. He was a Super Negro! His work ethic was amazing; his strength and energy matched that of any 21-year-old. His common-sense know-how put him on the same intellectual level as the so-called engineers.

As for the rest of us, we all had some college or trade school backgrounds. Not all were graduates but all of us had gone to school beyond high school. As for the

Whites, most were lucky to have gotten out of grammar school. Of course, I don't have any proof of that, but I'm just saying, many of them acted "as dumb as nails" to me.

Rich Black worked for the Mills for a long time. The White supervisors put a handle to his name and called him "Mr. Rich" or Mr. Black. He was promoted to head of maintenance and assistant facilities manager because the White facilities manager would never have known what size screws or light bulbs to buy without asking him.

All that goodness, hard work, and dedication to the White man's job and what had it gotten him? I'll bet that Mr. Black's paycheck was less than half that of those sorry White boys who didn't know their behinds from a hole in the ground.

During any given workday Mr. Black could be found doing things guys half his age wouldn't touch. One day for example, I walked into the mill to see the seventy-year old Mr. Black perched at the top of a 20- foot ladder fiddling with the skylight. He was retrieving a bird's nest with baby birds inside. Another day I found him flat on his back with only his feet stickin' out of the concrete dock. When I yelled down to ask him, "Hey Mr. Rich, what are you doing down there?"

He calmly replied, "There is oil leaking from this thing and I am trying to see where it is coming from." The thing he was talking about was a fully loaded, 18-foot trailer. Never mind that a white mechanic was paid to routinely check and repair vehicles.

Of course, Cone Mills never compensated or acknowledged what he did. Everybody respected Mr. Rich as the resident Christian counselor, mediator and all-around gentleman. I can only imagine how much money he saved the company because of his wisdom, decency, and honor. It makes me think of the scripture in Colossians 3:23-24. Read it in your own Bible and see if you agree with me.

One of Mr. Black's favorite teachings was, "Give your best to the world, and the best will come back to you." Mr. Rich always had special words of wisdom for me. I think that was because he had watched my daddy grow up and was now seeing me. The thing he would say to me more than anything else was, "Son, you gotta let that anger go. It's eating you alive and you don't even realize it. I can see it son."

I would never really respond to him. His voice was a reminder of the Holy Spirit keeping me on the right track. One day he caught me off guard, "I see you sitting out there on the rail when I come in to work, you look mad enough to eat a nail! What you so mad at?" He tousled my hair and put a caring arm around my shoulder. "I don't know if an old man like me can tell you much, but I can sure listen. Stop by my office first chance you get and let's talk about what's eating you." He called to my back as I started to walk away, "Don't wait too long, now."

I laughed over my shoulder, "Your office is a glorified janitor's closet. All you have in there is a desk and chair surrounded by a dozen mops, pails and brooms. After all your loyalty to Cone Mills, they didn't even have the decency to give you a real office."

A few weeks after our conversation, Mr. Black was found dead of a heart attack in his car. He had apparently left the building, gone to his car and started to put his keys into the ignition. He never made it out of the parking lot. I wonder if my life would have been different if I had gone to his office for that talk.

When the time came to plan Mr. Rich's funeral there was no money. The mill offered no life insurance or pension benefits to Negro workers. I am not sure if the White employees had burial insurance. Brother Black had a life insurance policy which he had carried for forty years, but they didn't have a health plan.

It was shocking to me when our pastor beckoned for me and several other men to come into his study following a Sunday service. "Ya'll know that Brother Black and his wife have been pillars of this church forever. They would take food off their own table and clothes off their backs to help somebody else." He had been working with Sister Black and Brown's Funeral Home to work out a payment plan. The mortician, who knew every Colored family in town, had lowered the cost as much as possible.

He looked around the room at all of us, "Ya'll know, too that Brother Black was no slouch when it came to taking care of his responsibilities. He always aimed to do the right thing; somehow things did not go right for him."

We all shook our heads in agreement. One of the Deacons spoke up, "When Sister Black developed breast cancer, they used the cash from their life policy to pay for her cancer treatments."

Pastor chimed in, "So what I'm asking you, brothers, is that we first have a word of prayer and then pass this offering basket around to help this family. We need $500 for a down payment and $1,000 in six months. Brown's has agreed to put Mr. Black away handsomely if we can come up with the money. I know that if Brother Rich were standing here instead of any one of us, he'd be the first to help."

Pastor began to pray, "…and God, as You have instructed us to care for the widows…" Silently, he placed a handwritten personal check for $300 into the basket. I added $200 for me and Dot. Everybody in the room gave all they could afford to show our love and respect for Mr. Richard Black.

At his funeral service a week later, a handful of White supervisors and coworkers from the Mill showed up to say kind things about him. One referred to him as "the gentle giant, a soft-spoken voice of wisdom housed in a long, lean body." Someone else talked about how many disputes, fights or firings he had averted with calm words of wisdom. The man recounted that Mr. Black had said, "Listen to me Son, is that worth your job?"

Not one of the flowery words came with a check to compensate him for or offer of assistance. Mr. Rich Black's death left me with a sinking feeling that I could not seem to shake. It was reminiscent of the feeling I experienced when I passed Brown's Funeral Home. I hated every day after Mr. Rich's death, that I had to walk inside that Mill.

For most people at the Mill, the day after Mr. Rich Black's funeral was business as usual. It had to have been one of the worst days of my life. I felt sick to my stomach, my head ached, and I could not talk to anybody.

At some point during the days following Mr. Rich's death, I was sitting alone at a table in the breakroom. I realized that he was the latest in a string of mentors following Jackie Robinson whom God had intentionally brought into my life. These mentors and father figures would teach me valuable lessons which I, in turn, would teach to others. ***Then the light came on.***

I left the breakroom feeling oddly detached from my surroundings. I completed the last leg of my tour and joined workers who had been lackadaisical about punching in. We anxiously shoved and pushed our way to punch out and start supper break promptly at 7:30. Behinds and backs were tired from four hours of sitting. Feet, legs and arms ached from non-stop walking, standing and pushing. Minds were exhausted and ready for a mental break.

Although it seemed insignificant, supper break was a major stressbuster. From the clock there was a beeline to the restrooms and from there to the cheerfully colored and brightly lit break room located in the south corner of the building. The room was spotless and inviting thanks to the good-looking Mac and Katie McDougal. They were a hardworking Negro couple in their early fifties who had been hired to manage food services. We all know they took their job seriously.

Along one wall of the lunchroom was an aluminum table that held a mini- refrigerator, a warmer, and a toaster oven. There was space to prepare your food and a beverage center with hot or cold drinks. There was a cooler for ice-cream bars and popsicles and Katie fired up an electric popcorn popper during breaks. Of course, there were the not-so-healthy snacks available in vending machines.

The tables and chairs were neatly arranged to seat two, four, six or twelve. Whether you wanted to sit alone and read a book, socialize with friends or play a game of Bid Whist there was a table for you. Mac and Katie thought of everything. They were professionals who loved their job and did it well. They would expand this service and move their food services into other mills. Cone Mills would recognize the entrepreneurial efforts of this young Negro family and would encourage them to continue, Right?

Wrong! Less than a year after I left Cone Mills, Dot shared with me that Mac and Katie had won a contract to provide food service at the Post Office similar to what they were doing at Cone Mills. Shortly after that expansion Mac had a minor car accident that left his leg in a cast. Cone Mills cancelled their contract alleging that Mac was physically unable to perform at two facilities. They took the position that Katie could not do it alone. That was another sickening blow to the pit of my stomach!

When quitting time finally arrived on Friday May 29, 1959 there would be an adrenalin rush and a mad stampede toward the time clock. We herded through the quadruple bumper doors and into the parking lot. The smell of weekend was exhilarating to everyone!

Physical fatigue added to the constant pressure to make production, keep moving and remain laser focused was relentless. It was a silent killer, most of us did not even realize we were "inside that pressure cooker" until it was too late. That was when guys would go home and abuse the wives and kids. We would have too much to drink and crash into telephone poles; kill someone in a fit of rage or simply fall dead of a heart attack. That was the harsh reality of life in the mills.

People dropped their inside voices and bellowed from one car to another, "Whatcha' got going on this weekend? Anything or nothing?"

Somebody would holler, "Let me have that guy's phone number. I want to have him look at my car."

Comradery could be heard throughout the parking lot, "I know you've got a six-pack in your trunk. Let me have one."

Some folk broke into song. Others rough-housed and pushed at each other, playfully. Adding credibility to quitting time was the whistle of a midnight train blowing as it passed the mill each night. The crowd was rowdy, the atmosphere, celebratory. Colored men and women were jubilant to be alive, to have jobs, transportation and to have completed another day.

Not everybody went straight home after work. Some would stop by the pool hall or by liquor houses. I did not know it then, but this would be the last time I would ever set foot inside Cone Mills. When my shift began on Monday, June 1, 1959 I would be noticeably absent.

PART II: SOMETHING I DID NOT DESERVE

Out of My Body -- Out of My Mind

I have a friend who was in World War II. He told me how he was on a mission and picked up a helmet. He told me, "I saw a decapitated head inside that helmet. I couldn't move. I couldn't breathe." I can still remember the look on his face as he described holding the helmet.

"What were you thinking?"

My friend replied, "In my mind, I wondered where the rest of the body was. I was caught between two worlds. It was an out of body experience."

You do still remember me telling you about my birth in the little house on Benbow Road, right? Remember how I kept seeing faces and hearing voices? How people bumped into each other and how furniture swirled through the air? Remember how desperately, from the dresser drawer, I tried to make somebody notice me? How I was never able to connect to the moment? In that dresser drawer, I was having an out of body experience. My body was in one plane while the spirit and soul were in a totally different one.

I was having another out of body experience. Just as I had the day I was born. I was watching a gruesome murder unfold in front of my eyes, and I was powerless to stop it! From a black .38 caliber pistol came POP! POP! POP! POP! POP! in rapid succession.

The five pops sounded like fire crackers. They were so loud, they deafened me. For a second, four eyes met and locked. Two souls mirrored each other. The rage, vengeance and unforgiveness in my eyes met deceit and manipulation in the other. I saw something in those eyes that made me pull the trigger.

I knew something about the man that I had promised to never reveal. Although I vowed not to be influenced by hearsay, seeing him turned me into a person I could not control. From widened eyes, more white than black, a stream of blood trickled downward to merge with blood bubbling from the nostrils and ears.

There was choking, gurgling and gagging. Blood from the eyes, ears, nose and mouth ran together and puddled at the chin before dripping onto the starched, white shirt of the Greensboro City Police uniform. Then the entire front of the shirt was red. Blood dripped onto the badge.

As the deafening sirens of police squad cars and emergency vehicles pierced the midnight silence, something fell and hit the floor with a thud. A body racked with convulsions fell with arms flailing and legs kicking uncontrollably. Then for one final second, two pairs of eyes met. A barely audible plea from the barely moving lips of one man to the barely feeling soul of another "Mer? Cee?"

Then I entered this great abyss. It was vast, dark and dismal. Time and place all ran together. I have no idea what happened next...or next...or next... That's where I stayed for a long time. I know that it was Monday, June 1, 1959.

In the late 1950s cop killings nor black-on-black crimes had not reached epidemic proportions. This story was probably one of the first of its kind. Television, radio and newspaper reporters from around the state picked it up, each one added a sensational slant to the story:

"City Police Officer is Shot and Killed"
Greensboro Daily News
Monday, June 1, 1959

"[Saturday night] A Greensboro officer gave a taxi driver a ticket for obstructing traffic near the campus of A&T College on West Market Street. The taxi driver, Joseph Daniel Herring, Jr. got back at the officer by killing him . . ."

***

"Massey was shot five times in the chest at Foust Service Station ..."

One article painted me as "heartless, cold-blooded and zombie-like."

Another said, "Herring showed no remorse. Had no feelings for Massey's two young children who were now double orphans. They lost their mother to cancer a short time earlier."

"Sergeants E. R. Medbury and Henry Evans, who investigated the shooting, said that Herring told them Cpl. Massey gave him a ticket for double parking shortly after midnight when he let a drunken passenger out ...."

"...this is what Herring told them about the events leading up to the shooting: Herring went to his home on Julian Street, got a box of cartridges from a dresser drawer and a pistol from under the mattress where his wife was sleeping. He awakened his wife and said, "Goodbye Baby. Wake up the children and tell them goodbye. I'm going to kill a man."

"Herring then went back to the taxi stand {also} on Market Street and waited for Massey to pass on his routes. When he had waited about 15 minutes without seeing Massey, he walked …a block and saw the officer inside Foust's Service Station. There were several others in the station. Herring waited for them to leave, went inside and shot Massey, six times at close range."

"Negro Cab Driver Kills Negro Cop"
Jet Magazine, June 18, 1959
Page 46

"In Greensboro, NC, a Negro Cab Driver is being held without bond for first-degree murder in the death of a Negro police officer. Joseph D. Herring, the cabbie, was allegedly upset because Cpl. Joseph Massey gave him a traffic ticket for double parking. Herring allegedly said later, that he only double parked for a minute and that was to allow a -drunk passenger to get out of his cab in front of his own doorstep. "Had I put him out even a half block farther, he could never have found his way home."

"According to one article, the second passenger in Herring's taxi at the time of the ticketing gave this account:

I was sitting in the back seat. Joe wanted to make sure Slick made it into his house okay. Next thing I saw was this brother, a police officer, standing by Joe's window talking. I could not hear what either man was saying but there was no argument. I saw the officer give Joe a piece of yellow paper, that looked like a ticket. Joe politely accepted and said nothing.

As the officer turned and headed back to his squad car with blue lights flashing, Joe looked at the ticket, tossed it onto his dashboard and then leaned out his window and yelled, 'Hey, Mr. Massey, may I speak with you?'

Officer Massey did not answer or even acknowledge that he had heard the question. We pulled off and proceeded around the corner to my house. I got out of the taxi, paid my 35-cent fare and went inside. Joe drove off. I thought that was the end of it. I could hardly believe my eyes when I got to church and heard the news or when I saw it in the paper.

***

"Officer's slaying described" . . .

Testimony was completed in four hours yesterday after it had taken two and a half days to pick a jury. The all-male jury of eight Whites and five Negroes including an alternate was sequestered and housed at two local motels.

73

"Herring, a 31-year old mill worker and part-time cab driver, is being held in Guilford Superior Court for murder in connection with the death of Cpl. Joseph R. Massey, also a Negro, and a 12-year veteran of the police department. The defendant allegedly shot Massey, 41, after the officer gave him a traffic ticket earlier that night."

"Herring is Given Life for Murder of Police Officer" GREENSBORO DAILY NEWS Thursday, July 9, 1959

"Herring pleaded innocent but did not testify. The defense rested its case without calling in a single character witness. Four witnesses for the state testified that Herring told them he 'shot Massey, was glad he did it and he hoped the officer would die.'"

***

The Greensboro Record

The Record Is In Its 72nd Year	Greensboro, N. C., Monday Evening,	Thirty-Two Pages

Herring is Given Life for Murder of Greensboro Police Officer

The owners of the service station, A. Foust, and J. Clark said they saw Herring empty a .38 caliber pistol on Massey, who was sitting on a stool at a desk inside Foust's Market Street Station. Foust said, "Clark and I were in the station getting ready to close up. Massey was at the desk making out his police report. Herring came in the door, called him by name and started shooting."

Foust, a short, stocky man reenacted the shooting with such convincing accuracy that people in the courtroom nearly fell out of their chairs trying to dodge bullets. Some worried that Foust might suffer a heart attack as he threw his obese body onto the floor, emulating what happened to the fallen officer.

When Foust reached that part in his role where the officer was struck by the first bullets, he slumped over in the witnesses' chair in such a realistic swoon that a white-haired deputy sheriff rushed over to assist him. Before the officer could reach him, Foust staggered down in front of the jury and hit the floor with a thud, sending gasps throughout the courtroom.

One police detective described the event as "one of the most classic cases of cold-blooded, pre-meditated murder he had ever witnessed." Another officer quoted me as having said, "I'm glad he is dead. I aimed to kill him. Now, my execution will be quick, and I will be dead, too."

Those days inside the Guilford County Superior Courthouse were a blur. I was in a stupor, so none of it made sense to me. When I got the chance to see my wife and my three beautiful babies, in that tiny room off to the side of the courtroom, I couldn't feel or speak. I saw the hurt, shock, disbelief and fear in their eyes. I saw four sets of big, beautiful eyes brimming with tears.

Dot's heart, along with the children's hearts beat wildly; my baby girl sobbed out loud; my older daughter cried without making a sound as she turned her face away from me. My son. Oh, God, my son! His little face looked just like mine. His wide, innocent eyes pleaded with me to go home with him.

I stared at these four people whom I loved more than anything in the world, but I could not speak. The newspapers had it right. They said I was a ghost. Sitting in that concrete cubicle, with its walls painted green, was a man devoid of a soul. There sat an empty shell, posing as me. He was exactly my size dressed in a pair of khakis and a white tee shirt and had slight stubble on his face.

The bailiff opened the heavy, steel door and nodded to indicate that visitation time was over. I had been counseled that it would be less traumatic for the children if they walked away from me as opposed to my walking away from them. I motioned for Dot to leave the room with them while I stayed seated at the steel, gray table.

They made it almost to the door before that plan went awry. Inches away from the red exit sign, they turned abruptly and ran back toward me. I scrambled, awkwardly to get up from the table and embraced them, as if to shield them from the unfathomable pain and shame they were about to walk into.

I cupped Dot's face and looked into her eyes. Through her tears I saw that same trust and admiration for me that I remembered from the magic show the first time we met. What a disappointment I must have been to her! With trembling hands, I stroked her hair back, kissed her forehead and her lips. I looked in her eyes and said, "You have always been my strength. Instead of grabbing the gun and going to seek revenge I wish I had climbed into bed beside you. Our lives may never have reached this point." I squeezed her so tightly that I nearly broke her in half.

Next, cupping each little face with my hand, I looked into the eyes of each of my three children and prayed for the right words. Drawing in a deep breath, I spoke slowly, "Daddy has done something bad and now, he has to suffer the consequences for that sin. That means leaving you for a time."

Joey didn't understand, "Daddy, will you come back to see my game? You say I've got a good arm. Don't you want to see me pitch?" In that second, my life flashed back twenty-five years. That was when I had uttered the identical plea to my dad, "Will you be back for my game?"

Looking into the innocent eyes of my mini-me, I doubled over in pain! It was the same pain I had experienced whenever I passed Brown's Funeral Home. It was the same pain I had experienced when I sucked in my breath and longed, desperately to hear my Dad say, "Sure,

Son, I'll be there." Incidentally, I never heard those words and I could not say them to my own son in that moment.

I hesitated again as I thought of the words of my friend, Mr. Rich. He said to me, many times, "Joe, people are not always going to give you what you want, what you need or even what you deserve from them. That does not make them bad people. People can't give you what they don't have. Sometimes they may have it but not know how to give it. It's just not always as easy as it seems, my Boy. One day the switch will flip, and you will understand what I'm saying."

As the five of us stood sobbing together inside that icy, green room, my head began to spin, my rubbery legs gave way. Sweat poured from my body. I slid down to the concrete floor into a puddle of something wet. Grown men don't faint, do they?

"God, how did I get here?" I screamed aloud. I literally felt my soul re-enter my body. My conscience and all my emotions had left my body at the beginning of this nightmare. I could sense my body reconnecting with my spirit. Things were coming into focus. Reality was kicking in. I was sitting in jail, awaiting trial for murder. Did I even dare, let alone, deserve to ask for mercy?"

> *"Let us draw near with confidence to the throne of grace, that we may receive mercy and may find grace to help in time of need."*
> *Hebrews 4:16*

He Gave Me Mercy

I sat on the lumpy cot inside the jail cell trying to figure out what was really happening. So far, that was not working. God]gave me grace. I had neither earned it nor deserved it, but He gave it to me anyway.

If you had heard my story three and a half decades ago you would have assumed that the "he" in my story was Corporal Joe Massey and the "something I did not deserve" was a traffic ticket. Your assumption would have been right! Praise God, I learned to share my story from a totally different paradigm. The "He" I am talking about this time is God and the "something" I did not deserve is "mercy."

> *"for by grace you have been saved...and that not of yourselves; it is the gift of God..."*
> *Ephesians 2:8-9*

Maybe men do faint. But maybe "knocked out" sounded more macho, because that was how the guard explained where I had been for the last thirty-six hours. I awakened to the aroma of freshly brewed coffee, fried pork sausage, eggs and grits. For the first time in I don't know how long, I was hungry. Actually, I was starved! Still disoriented and vague about my surroundings, I gave a polite "Good morning" and "Thank you, Sir" to the man handing me a brown, plastic tray of food. It smelled so enticing and I was ready to devour it.

The man responded, "You are welcome, Mr. Herring. Enjoy your breakfast. Someone will be here to talk with you shortly."

Someone will be where? To talk with me about what? I was too hungry to think about it. As the nice man set the food on one end of my cot, he indicated with a sweeping hand-motion that I was to sit on the other end.

He looked at me with compassion, and spoke, "Again, Mr. Herring, I am sorry, but I have to do it this way. It's my job." I had no idea what he was talking about until I had taken my first gulp of wonderful, black coffee and followed it with a mouthful of hot, buttered grits. The awful sound of a heavy, iron gate clanging into position; the loud click of a locking key, followed by the clang of a second, solid iron door as it slid across a track in the concrete floor and banged shut against the opposite wall jolted me into harsh reality. That sound of that closing door is one I will never forget as long as I live!

Hot grits and coffee spewed from my mouth. Eggs, sausage and whatever else was left on the tray careened across the floor as I jumped up from the bed. There was a clang, then the jingle of keys turning and locking the doors with me behind bars!

A bolt, like lightning hit me, jolting me onto the floor, then back onto my feet again. Bells rang in my ears and stars flashed across my eyes! *Then the light came on!* I was in jail. I didn't know what day or what time it was. I wasn't sure where Dot and the kids were.

At first, I wasn't sure why I was there, but as the light grew brighter it illuminated not only the cell, but also my mind. I had shot and killed a policeman for what seemed, according to news reports, like no reason at all — a parking ticket that would have cost me one dollar and forty cents! They did not know my story, and until that moment, neither did I. I could not have told you why I was so mad or so mean. Not until the light bulb came on in that jail cell on June 3, 1959 did I begin to see the revelation.

I remembered Mama Sallie teaching multiplication and long division. She had me memorize Bible verses while

80

I shot marbles. I remembered her kissing my scraped knees and arms when I was seven or eight and comforting me with her words when I felt embarrassed or insecure as a pre-teen.

I remembered her affirming words that I was "a good boy, smart, intelligent, tall, athletic, good-looking and fun to be around." She would wink and say, "All these little gals will be after you. No more talk about quitting or not being good enough. Brush yourself off and get back into the race. You are as good as the next guy. Remember that." Mama Sallie was as sweet as the God she sang about.

Thoughts flashed across my brain as I closed my eyes and tried to figure out all that was happening. Ever so slowly, it was coming back to me. Dot and the children had been told about the murder and had come to visit me. That meeting had been extremely hard. My pastor, my dad, my brothers, a court-appointed lawyer and a psychiatrist met with me.

Nobody came out and asked, but I am sure they were all thinking, "Joe, what were you thinking? Did you snap?" I would not have known the answers then, and thirty-five years later I still cannot give you a play-by-play as to what drove me to do what I did that night.

As I reflected on my life, I know that I have always been a complicated individual. I told you how my Dad described me as smart, too smart for my own good, hot headed and hot tempered.

Mr. Black from the Mill made a deep impression on me. I thought of how he said to me, "Joe, you are too thin-skinned. Get that chip off your shoulder and stop letting what folks do make you so mad. Don't you understand that every time you allow somebody to get under your skin, you allow them to control you?"

Some said I was strong-willed. Others said I was arrogant. Some called me honest, fair, proud and a perfectionist. One of my daughters referred to me as classy, well-dressed and handsome. One of my sisters called me selfish and egotistical, while another sister saw me as generous and supportive. Church members saw me as a generous giver, an organizer, strong leader and as a wise and gifted teacher.

My wife saw a side of me that nobody else was able to see. She always encouraged me, "You are a fierce protector of our family, and a loving and gentle husband and father."

As I sat on the cot in that jail cell thinking, nothing in life had ever come clearer to me. *And then the light came on!*

> *"I will give thanks to Thee, for I am fearfully and wonderfully made."*
> *Psalm 139:14*

They were all right. I was a bit of what everybody perceived of me. The most important thing was that I was exactly who God had created me to be. Every single perception of me whether good or bad would work together for my good as I walked into the purpose for which God had created me.

All of those complexities that were combined to make me were not by chance. Before I was born, God had orchestrated my life. While everybody else, including myself, was baffled by my behavior God was not shocked by anything. Everybody wanted to know: How could Joe? What led Joe? When did Joe? How did Joe? What was Joe thinking? God already knew that every triumph and every tragedy would position me for a greater purpose. That day marked both the ending and the beginning of Joseph Daniel Herring, as we all knew him.

***

Several weeks later, I would leave that cell and be escorted to the courthouse where Honorable Judge Walter Crissmon would sentence me to "spend the rest of my natural life in jail." For a few more days after sentencing, there were a few more precious hours with Dot, Pat, Lynda and Joey with tears, hugs and kisses.

There were a few more conversations with my lawyers. Attorney Lee was one of the most prominent Black lawyers in the state. He and his partner Stanback talked about appeals. After that, I was transferred to Raleigh and given a new address, the Department of Federal Corrections ... and a new name: #073 492.

> *" given a new address, the Department of Federal Corrections ... and a new name: #073 492"*

Prison was a radical adjustment for me. I went in with many of the same attitudes that I had held for the past thirty-one years. I was angry at anybody and everybody! I was bitter, with or without cause. My imprisonment did not necessarily begin when I moved to Raleigh.

It did not take long to find out that there were others there who were as angry, as bitter and as rejected as I felt. I had a lot to learn. Although I had previous run ins with the law, I was always let out by God's mercy. Shortly after moving to Greensboro, I had been arrested and accused of being part of a riot and street fight. Remember, I had also gotten into a fight at Ham Fat's.

During my first year, I had several interactions with other inmates, but it must have been Mama Sallie's prayers that kept my temper intact. Dot told me that she squeezed her hands and prayed fervently for me:

83

"God take care of my boy inside those walls. They say that he confessed to killing that policeman. I know he didn't mean to do these bad things.

Lord, let me live long enough to see his face one more time before I leave this earth. Keep this family together. Let us keep loving one another no matter how bad we mess up. Teach us how to forgive one another just as You have forgiven us. You know he's got a temper. Don't let nobody down there hurt him and don't let him hurt nobody. This is Sallie Carroll, mother to Joseph Herring. Thank You and Amen."

Serving My Time

I told you the newspapers and radio reporters made a big deal about my saying that the cop had given me something I did not deserve. The media made a laughing stock out of me. "What evil idiot literally kills someone over a traffic ticket?"

I was portrayed as a blabbering imbecile, saying "yah, yah, I did it. Yeah, 'cause he gave me something I did not deserve." That was the height of my shame and humiliation and those words "…gave me something I didn't deserve" reverberated within me for years.

Fast forward three or four years, *then the light came on* and I finally "got it." I got the lesson God was trying to teach me. He had even used Mr. Rich to hammer that point into my thick head. "Don't complicate life by trying to determine what's fair or not fair, deserved or undeserved. That's not your job. Just find God's plan for your life, align yourself with that and He will do the rest." It took four years of being away for me to get it.

I found myself repeating Mr. Black's words to some of the fellas in prison with me. Many were mad about circumstances they could not control. Just as I had done, they saw themselves as victims. They were always on the defensive, always needing to get even.

I was thirty-five years and a lot younger than some of the other guys. Many of them had been there for fifteen or twenty years and had little hope of ever getting out. "With this mindset," I said to a group of them, "you're either kicking somebody else's behind or looking back to see if someone is about to kick yours."

I felt the call to talk to other prisoners about the life lessons I had learned the hard way. I had made some bad choices, but if my words could reshape their thinking, there was a lesson in my losses. This is what mercy looks like. I thought about my life and realized everything had been for His specific purpose.

I can't tell you when, but at some point, I became overwhelmed by a calm reassurance. Changes in my thinking and my behavior did not go unnoticed. I would see guards watching me and studying my reactions. The teachings of Mr. Rich and my Grandpa Herring began to flow out of me. I found myself repeating many of their words. I told someone like Grandpa Herring had told me, "I don't care why you are here or what you have done, there's a lesson in it. Learn it."

In my nine years being incarcerated, I never missed a visitor's call. Between Dot and the kids; my Pa, my siblings and their kids, I never lacked visitors. Unfortunately, Mama Sallie was never in that number. They offered to pick her up in Elizabethtown and take her to Raleigh, but she adamantly refused every invitation.

Dot said at the mention of my name, Mama Sallie's big, pretty brown eyes would get watery and she would clutch her heart and say in a heart wrenching wail, "Lord, Lord, where did I go wrong? I just can't see my son locked up like that. I know I would just drop dead right on the spot!" Dot could not stand to see Mama Sallie moaning and shaking uncontrollably. It hurt her heart.

For the first few years, I called Mama Sallie for Christmas, Mother's Day and her birthday, but she got so upset that I stopped calling. For more than ten years, we neither saw each other nor heard the other's voice. We kept in touch through weekly letters. She would slip in juicy news clippings from the *Bladen County Review* about people I had grown up with or those that Mama Sallie thought I should know. People like Don Frye, the first African American to be elected to North Carolina's House of Representatives and Basal Spaulding, founder of North Carolina Mutual Insurance Company had gone ahead to

86

make names for themselves. There were people who had grown up with me who made headlines for less notable reasons. Mama Sallie sent obituaries of those who died of natural causes and those who died from unfortunate stabbings or shootings.

As the days changed to months and years my heart softened. I learned to surrender to the Anointing. He did not leave me. Thanks be to God; my story did not end there!

"The prison in which they placed Joseph became his stepping-stone to the palace for which God had destined him. ..."
The Word for You Today Daily Devotional
Celebration Inc.
Sept/Oct/Nov 2018 edition, p. 10.

Mansion Duty

After a while the inmates began to ask me to help mediate their disputes. I guess I learned that from Mr. Rich who was said to have averted many disputes and arguments at the mill. His "do unto others as you would have them do unto you message" was one of my lessons in mercy.

To my surprise in 1964 I was summoned by the warden. "Prisoner Herring, I have a special assignment for you. Governor Moore needs a man to attend to his garden and grounds. We see your work around here and we trust that you would be the man for the job."

I was stunned. It had only been four years into my sentence. I heard him say, "How do you feel about that? He needs a head gardener who can teach the others how the work should be done. We trust you and we want to promote you to the high position of Trustee."

I didn't know what to say. ***Then the light came on*** and once again I heard the voice of the Anointing say to me, "You will be a teacher like no other. The lessons you teach will come from your experiences."

The special assignment meant that I would have special quarters inside the mansion. I could move out of my tiny cell! I wanted to stay connected to the guys I met. I asked the warden, "May I be able to attend anger management classes with them?" Not only did he agree to that, some were released under my care to work with me at the mansion.

My special assignment at 200 North Blunt Street in Raleigh, North Carolina was a great lesson in mercy and a key step toward my destiny. For the next four years I served under Governors Dan K. Moore and Terry Sanford. Like Joseph in the Bible, the governors saw leadership in me and took favor on me. I took care of the grounds, cooked, and worked in the kitchen for state dinners and other big events. I loved taking care of the flowers. It reminded me of Mama Sallie who had instilled a love of gardening in me.

For the last two years of my prison term, I was able to visit my family in a conference room off the mansion. My Pa and my siblings came to see me and Dot would bring the children. I looked forward to having intimate time with all of them. Even though I was missing a great part of their life, I could thank God for a degree of normalcy with my precious family.

My daughter Pat and I would read the same books and talk about them. I always challenged the children in my life to read. my niece, Donna, especially liked the challenge. Lynda always made me smile with her big hugs. I saw such great potential in all of them.

I was most excited that my son could see me in a different light. They said they were not ashamed of me, but I could not imagine how they would not be. Joey looked at me through the eyes of love as only a kid could, "Daddy, you really live here?"

***

Four and a half years in the mansion went fast. Through God's mercy, I did my due diligence and before I knew it there was talk of my getting out early. I had only

90

served for nine years. My lawyers Stanback and Lee were faithful to their word of checking on me. They stayed in constant contact with Governor Moore on my behalf. Eventually, their efforts were successful, and he approved a pardon for me. On December 31, 1964, my life sentence was commuted to fifty years. In December of 1965, my sentence was commuted to 43 years.

"The slain police officer was neither the first nor the only one to lose his life in the process of giving me something I didn't deserve!

The slain police officer was neither the first nor the only one to lose his life in the process of giving me something I didn't deserve!

LESSONS IN MERCY

PART III: NEW BEGINNING

Official Pardon

I was shaking like a leaf as the kind, Bailiff led me to a room in the courthouse. The sign on the door said, "Parole Hearings." Attorney Lee who was waiting outside the door with Attorney Stanback, asked, "So, are you ready for this?" I nodded my head in affirmation, "Good. Take a deep breath and let's do it."

The Bailiff waited a few moments before opening the door and leading us inside. When those heavy, double doors opened, I felt as if I were stepping into heaven! Between my two brothers, Richard and Wray, Dot sat, looking like an angel. I couldn't stop my tears from flowing or my feet from trying to run toward her.

"Hold on." the nice bailiff redirected my steps toward a table in the opposite direction where I sat between my lawyers.

There was a flurry of activities reminiscent of the day I was born. People and furniture were floating around in the air while I lay swaddled in a towel in a dresser drawer. I heard people talking about me, but not to me. That day I heard words like, "Exhibit 1", "good behavior" and "obligation to the state of North Carolina."

There was a lot of conversation back and forth between my lawyers and the Parole Board. Finally, there was the thunder of the gavel followed by the authoritative voice of the judge saying, "Parole granted!

Nearly 90 days passed before the official documents were signed and I was free to go home. On the morning of my big day, I got up earlier than usual to take a final grand promenade around the gorgeous 5-acre garden of the Governor's mansion. A ring of pink and white dogwood trees outlined the edge of the property. The view was spectacular in my eyes!

Interspersed among and towering above them were magnolias, red maples and crepe myrtles. Below those were azaleas. Finally, at ground level were 150 hues and varieties of annuals like peonies, heather and jonquils. Did I mention that several extra-large gazebos, numerous birdbaths and a fish pond completed the picture? I smiled as I thought to myself, *"Mama Sallie would be pleased to see that her green thumb, her passion for beautiful lawns and gardens and all the lessons she had taught me about landscaping has paid off."*

I don't know how long I stayed out that morning, reflecting, praying and thanking God for His mercies. As I started back to my living quarters, I got a call on my Walkie-Talkie from my Supervisor. "Joe, come on over here to the kitchen. A few of your co-workers have something to tell you."

"Yessir. Just give me a few minutes to freshen up. I just finished my morning jog. "
Before I could get to the kitchen, the Head Chef and a few other staffers, with funny looking grins on their faces, re-directed me. "Come this way."

I followed them to one of the small dining rooms. We entered a room across from the magnificent ballroom where state dinners were held. The room was filled with people. There were balloons and flowers from my special garden in front of Dot. The seat beside her had been left for me. My Attorneys Lee and Stanback along with my three brothers Richard, Wray and Jeff were all there too.

For a full hour I was awe stricken at the love shown to me. The mansion chef, with whom I had become good friends and prayer partners had prepared my favorite meal of filet mignon, baked potato and his special chef salad. I shook my head in amazement. An imprisoned man could only get his favorite meal on the night before he was to be executed. God had been merciful to me!

As we enjoyed brunch, Blacks, Whites, old and young, free and imprisoned men, inside and outside staff members gave comments from the podium. They wished me well, prayed for my life and thanked God for having allowed our lives to touch. Nearly everybody said that I had impacted their lives by something I had said or done. Everybody's remarks humbled me and brought tears to my eyes, but nobody got to me like the man who spoke on behalf of my "Dirty Dozen."

These were twelve inmates: three White, 2 Hispanic, 1 Native American and six Negro. The youngest was 19 and oldest was 67. Some serving short sentences and some serving life . "When we first came here to work with Mr. Joe," the designated spokesman said, "we called ourselves the *dirty dozen.* We were working in the dirt and we had some nasty, stinking attitudes and habits." He paused for laughter. "Thanks to this great teacher and man of God, we no longer feel dirty." The audience clapped. "He taught us to sing to the plants and how to manicure the lawn with a pair of nail clippers. More importantly, he taught us how to trim bitterness and hatred from our lives. Thank you, Mr. Herring."

My Supervisor walked to the podium. "Joe and Dot can you join me?" Nervously, we made our way to the front as he looked toward someone at the back of the room and said, "Where's that certificate we had for Joe? Did I leave it someplace?" Naturally everybody turned around to see who my Supervisor was talking to, then the room exploded with applause when to our surprise, Governor Dan Moore walked into the room.

He shook my hand and gave Dot a hug before speaking into the microphone, "When a man is incarcerated and loses his freedom, he takes his family with him. By the same token, when he regains his freedom, so does his family. Congratulations Mr. and Mrs. Herring." He handed

97

me an oversized pair of clippers, "Here, take these with you, Joe."

Never during my time at Central Prison nor during the years when I worked on special assignment at the Governor's Mansion had I seen a prisoner given this kind of honor. All I could say was, "Thank You, God for holding back Your wrath. Thank You for bringing me here to this prison and for teaching me the lessons You wanted me to learn. But more than anything thank You for giving me something I did not deserve!"

> "... thank You for giving me something I did not deserve!"

By God's mercy I was released from prison in 1968. At that point, I had served fewer than ten years of what had started as a life sentence. Remember the Judge declared: "The rest of your natural life in jail . . ."

***

On the drive from Raleigh to Greensboro I took in the fresh air and the warm, winter sun. I smiled and listened as my brother, Richard excitedly, filled me in on what I had missed over the last decade. I squeezed Dot's thigh and pulled her close to me in the back seat. She wore a pale blue shirt waist dress that made her look like a beautiful angel.

After a while, I put my head on the headrest, closed my eyes and allowed my thoughts to roam. The ninety-minute ride from Raleigh to Greensboro felt like heaven opened up. The weather was beautiful, and the trees were greener than I had ever seen! This was the first time I had been to Greensboro since I left. I took in the beauty of my new freedom.

WEATHER		North Carolina's
Partly Cloudy, Warm	**GREENSBORO DAILY NEWS**	Finest Newspaper
Expected High Today: 80		
TEMPERATURES YESTERDAY		18 Pages—Two Sections
High 80, Low, 48		
(Other Data, Page 1, Section A)		

| VOL. No. ★ | GREENSBORO, N. C., MONDAY MORNING | PRICE: 30¢ Twelve Cents, (& out state) |

Slayer Escapes Gas Chamber due to Mercy Recommendation

A jury of eight white men and five (one alternate) Negro men found Herring guilty of First-Degree Murder.

LEE, HIGH, TAYLOR & DANSBY
ATTORNEYS AT LAW
P. O. BOX 20027
GREENSBORO, N. C. 27420

April 26, 1972

KENNETH LEE
...IA. LEE
...OR B. HIGH
HERMAN L. TAYLOR
DAVID M. DANSBY, JR.
A. LEON STANBACK, JR.

OFFICES
107 NORTH MURROW BLVD.

TELEPHONE
(919) 272-8182

20428-41

The Honorable Robert W. Scott
Governor of the State of North Carolina
State Capital Building
Raleigh, North Carolina 27603

ATTENTION: Attorney Fred Morrison

Dear Mr. Morrison:

Purusant to our recent telephone conversation, I am submitting this communication to request an unconditional pardon for Mr. Joseph E. Herring.

Mr. Herring was convicted on May 31, 1959, of first degree murder. He subsequently served 9 years under the supervision of the Department of Correction. For approximately one-half the total time served in prison, Mr. Herring was a trustee and served in the Governor's mansion during the terms of Governors Moore and Sanford.

Mr. Herring was released from prison in 1968 and on March 21, 1972, he was issued a certificate of discharge from the State Board of Paroles. I am prepared to submit the appropriate affidavits upon request from your office.

Please let me know what further action I should take in this matter, so that Mr. Herring's citizenship may be restored to him.

Thank-you for your co-operation in this matter.

Very truly yours,

LEE, HIGH, TAYLOR & DANSBY

A. Leon Stanback, Jr.

RECEIVED
MAY 8 1972

ALS:bnw

100

State of North Carolina

Office of The Board of Paroles

DAN K. MOORE
GOVERNOR
MARVIN R. WOOTEN
CHAIRMAN

HOWARD HEPLER
MEMBER
WADE E. BROWN
MEMBER
FOIL ESSICK
ADMINISTRATIVE ASSISTANT

831 West Morgan Street

Raleigh 27602

December 1, 1967

MEMORANDUM TO: Governor Dan K. Moore

SUBJECT: Joseph Daniel Herring, C/M, Age 39
             Alph. # H 2751-410-20428-41 M

At the July, 1959, Term of the Guilford Superior Court the inmate was convicted of First Degree Murder and was sentenced to life in prison. He was received in prison on July 11, 1959. The life sentence was commuted to 50 years December 31, 1964. On December 29, 1965, the 50 year sentence was commuted to 48 years. The 48 year sentence was commuted to 43 years on December 12, 1966. His tentative release date is November 15, 1986.

The fingerprint record indicates that in January, 1956, the inmate was charged with affray with a deadly weapon, and the disposition is not shown.

According to our information, the inmate was given a ticket for a traffic violation by a colored police officer, Joe Massey, at Greensboro on May 31, 1959. The inmate went home, got his .38 caliber pistol and searched for Officer Massey. He found him at Foust Service Station and shot him six times.

The inmate was assigned to Mansion duty August 10, 1964.

Chairman
_____
Marvin R. Wooten

MRW:FE:jh

RECOMMENDATION: This inmate's sentence be reduced 8 years from 43 years to 35 years.

STATE OF NORTH CAROLINA

DEPARTMENT OF SOCIAL REHABILITATION AND CONTROL

831 W. MORGAN ST.   RALEIGH 27603

GEORGE W. RANDALL
SECRETARY

ROBERT W. SCOTT
GOVERNOR

BOARD OF PAROLES

June 2, 1972   WADE E. BROWN, CHAIRMAN
ROBERT WEINSTEIN, MEMBER
JOHN H. BAKER, JR., MEMBER
831 W. MORGAN ST.
829-3414

Mr. A. Leon Stanback, Jr.
Attorney at Law
P. O. Box 20027
Greensboro, North Carolina

Re: Joseph E. Herring 20428-41 MH

Dear Mr. Stanback:

    Your letter of April 26, 1972 to the office of Governor Robert W.
Scott concerning the case of the above named has been referred to this
office for investigation and reply.

    We are happy to advise that we are beginning an investigation at
this time looking towards the possibility of granting him a pardon of
forgiveness.

    You may be assured he will be shown every possible consideration.

                                Sincerely,

                                Wade E. Brown

WEB:MHH:bd

102

LEE, HIGH, TAYLOR & DANSBY
ATTORNEYS AT LAW
P. O. BOX 20027
GREENSBORO, N. C. 27420

J. KENNETH LEE
ALVIS A. LEE
MAJOR S. HIGH
HERMAN L. TAYLOR
DAVID M. DANSBY, JR.
A. LEON STANBACK, JR.

OFFICES
107 NORTH MURROW BLVD.

TELEPHONE
(919) 272-8182

June 5, 1972

The Honorable Robert W. Scott
Governor of the State of
North Carolina
State Capitol Building
Raleigh, North Carolina 27603

Attention: Attorney Fred Morrison

Dear Mr. Morrison:

Please advise as to the status of my unconditional
pardon request for Mr. Joseph D. Herring.

Thank you very much for your cooperation in this
matter.

Very truly yours,

LEE, HIGH, TAYLOR & DANSBY

A. Leon Stanback, Jr.

ALS:mgt

103

GEORGE W. RANDALL
SECRETARY

ROBERT W. SCOTT
GOVERNOR

BOARD OF PAROLES

June 13, 1972

WADE E. BROWN, CHAIRMAN
ROBERT WEINSTEIN, MEMBER
JOHN H. BAKER, JR., MEMBER
831 W. MORGAN ST.
829-3414

Mr. A. Leon Stanback, Jr.
Attorney at Law
P. O. Box 20027
Greensboro, N. C.

Re: Joseph D. Herring 20428-41

Dear Mr. Stanback:

Your letter of June 5, 1972 to·the office of Mr. Fred Morrison concerning
the case of the above named has been referred to this office for investigation.
and reply.

We wish to advise that, we are conducting an investigation at this
time looking towards the possibility of granting this subject a pardon
of forgiveness. When our report from the field has been received in
our office, we will place the matter before our Board for further consideration.

If we can be of further assistance to you, please to not hesitate to
call upon us.

Sincerely yours,

Robert Weinstein

RW:MHH:bd

Acknowledging My Purpose

"Unless the student has learned,
the teacher has not taught."
~Bruce Wilkinson

When I returned home in 1968 from Central Prison, my family and friends welcomed me with open arms. I loved Dot more than the day I had seen her on those bleachers. She had been my rock while I was away. I could not thank her enough for having loved me through the eyes of mercy.

Richard pulled into the driveway of a house on Sir Gallahad. I thought we were going to our house on Julian Street, but Dot had worked her magic again and bought a brand-new house. It was beautiful and I could not wait to put my touch on the lawn and yard. Let me tell you about a prank I played on Dot.

She knew I would get raving mad if someone in a passing car flipped cigarette butts or threw paper onto our lawn, but this was a funny thing to do. Dot is thoroughly convinced that a Hollywood producer moved backwards in time and sneaked into our backyard to film that scene. I had the same crazy idea from the movie.

Dot woke up one morning and walked into the cheerful, yellow kitchen of our home. She described that her eyes followed a ray of morning sunshine beaming through the windows, and bathing the pretty potted flowers on the sunporch, "I lifted my eyes to utter a prayer of thanksgiving. My heart was bursting with happiness as I thanked Him for bringing you home. I thanked God for the beautiful, brand new house and for another chance to get it right. I felt so good that morning that tears of joy welled up in my eyes and rolled down my face onto the new kitchen counter tops.

I squeezed my eyes together, took in a huge breath, and held it. I finally exhaled and opened my eyes and allowed them to travel toward the tree-lined edge of my beautifully landscaped and meticulously manicured Yard of the Month. Then wham! My eyes rested on the most ghastly-looking, and frightening sight I had ever seen in my life! How did that heaping mound of ugly stuff get in my beautiful yard?"

When I heard her scream from the kitchen it felt like she pierced the whole neighborhood. I heard her saying, "Joe! Joe, come here." She was running to the front door. "Look at what somebody has dumped in our yard!" She was standing on the front porch shaking like a leaf. I held back my laugh to keep the joke going longer.

I opened the storm door and gently pulled her back inside the house. "It's okay, Babe."

"No, it's not ok. Somebody just dumped a truckload of rubbish in our yard last night! Somebody who doesn't want us in this neighborhood must have…"

"No, it's nothing like that. I'll tell you how they got there Dot."

"What!" She was shrieking, "Do you know something about this!" Tears are gushing like a broken hydrant and she was stuttering!

In the midst of calming her down, she looked at my face then out the window. "Look at those doggone toilet seats out there."

I must have given it away with my deer-in-the-headlights look. Her expression changed. "You did this? Mr. Meticulous? Mr. Efficiency?"

I loved to hear her tell the story of the porcelain thrones. People could never stop laughing and invariably, somebody would ask, "So, Mother Dot, whatever happened to those toilet seats?"

She would politely respond by getting out of her chair, opening the drapes that led to the screened-in sunporch and direct their eyes toward our backyard. There would be a loud, corporate gasp followed by thunderous roars of laughter! One lady laughed so hard that she fell out of her chair. In my last days, I would hear her tell the story and I would vehemently dispute every word.

With the evidence in front of them, they would laugh harder. "No disrespect, Papa" someone would say, "I think she has got you on this one."

I would raise myself on my elbow and say, "Naw, that's not what happened at all."

Home to Mama Sallie

Dot didn't ask me any questions or make any suggestions. She just gave me the space she thought I needed. After being home a few days, my mind turned to my beloved Mama Sallie. I could hardly wait to get back down home to see her. She was in her mid-seventies and suffering from heart trouble and high blood pressure.

I dreamed of our first reunion. She would stand on her tip-toes and pretend that she was going to wash my mouth with lye soap if I didn't watch my language. Maybe she would push her pointer finger against the tip of my nose and say, "Boy, you don't ever get too big for me to whip, do you hear me?" I had rehearsed my confirming response to her question.

Ironically, the reunion did not happen as I had envisioned. I wanted our time to be private. I chose to delay my visit until I got my driver's license, car registration, and title in my name.

Dot was working at North Carolina National Bank and could not get a day off until the weekend. I didn't want to wait for her to join me. I picked a day and before she left for work that morning, we had a light breakfast. "I'll call you when I get there."

"Do you remember the directions?"

"Of course, I do Dot! You never forget your way home do ya?"

"Drive safely. I love you Joe."

There was a long, tight squeeze followed by "I love you, too, Baby."

We both pulled out of the driveway and went our separate ways. For Dot it was a nine-hour day in the accounting department. For me, it would be a long awaited, bittersweet reunion with the only mother I had ever known.

As I drove to see my beloved Mama Sallie, I thought about how God had meant me to be both a Herring and a Carroll. Long before little Carol Dianne Johnson and her parents left Bladen County, we played together at family gatherings. When she returned to visit family in Elizabethtown many years later as the well-known star, Diahann Carroll, proud family members gathered to see her. Mama Sallie bragged frequently about the smart, pretty, rich and famous daughter of her second cousin.

The year I returned home Diahann Carroll became famous as the first Negro to star in her own television show. Diahann was one of the earliest portrayals of a single mom struggling to raise a little Negro boy alone. I would always see Mama Sallie as Julia and myself as her son, an inquisitive kid with more questions than answers.

By the time I reached Mama Sallie's house I was nervous and happy.

***

Dot was surprised when she returned home after work to see me sitting on the couch in the den, "What are you doing back so soon?"

"I don't want to talk about it."

That was not good enough for Dot, she kept asking questions. "What happened? Is Mama Sallie sick? Did someone try to stop you?"

Seeing that she wasn't going to back off, I gave a big sigh "Mama Sallie is not sick. She is fine and as feisty as ever."

"What did she do when she saw you?" My annoyance with her barrage of questions gave way to a smile as I relived my reunion. "For starters, when she opened the wooden door and saw me, she got so excited

110

that she could not unlatch the screen. The first thing she said was, "Where is Dot?"

"Working." I talked Mama Sallie through the actions for ten minutes. "Just slow down, Mama. Push that little knob under the latch and that will open the door."

I took a deep breath and watched Dot watching me with wide eyes. "At last, she finally got the door open and we literally blew into each other's arms. We were laughing and crying like crazy. Whew! It felt so good!"

"So, why are you back so soon?"

"Mama told me, 'Go back to Greensboro and get Dot. Don't you dare come down here without her anymore! As a matter of fact, don't go anywhere without her anymore! You already left her long enough. Ten years! You've got to be somewhere so fast that you can't wait one more day for your wife to join you?"

Dot laughed heartily. "Wow, I wasn't expecting that Joe. Wow."

"I was busted by my Mama. Only a mother's love can tell you that you are wrong and still love you like you are the greatest person on earth." Mama Sallie loved my Dot as much as I did; I will forever be indebted to Dot. I guess Mama Sallie knew that too.

Great News Church

I returned to my home church to join my brother and his family. After a few years, God sent me to Great News Baptist Church with an assignment to be a teacher, a mentor, and a coach. Before I could be that to others, there were some things I needed to learn myself. I was beginning a new phase with a new house, my adult children and a second chance.

Great News Baptist Church was in its beginning stages, having just split with St. John, one of the city's largest and most influential Black churches. The fifteen or so families who chose to leave St. John to start their own church were gutsy in my eyes.

Joining Great News Baptist Church was my first opportunity to work my assignment. I was able to experience God's promise to teach. Dot and I did not leave St. John immediately after my release from Central Prison. We waited a little more than a year before deciding to join the other families. We were moved by their courage, humility, and obedience.

Many of the young families, like Sister Irene Thomas and her husband, confirmed for me in many conversations that God had positioned me to encourage and to teach others. Although Sister Thomas was the age of my children, her wisdom, which was beyond her years, helped me acknowledge my struggle with carrying a mantle of guilt and how I could get over it.

Sister Thomas enjoys telling the story of how we met before Bible study one day:

"I had been a member of Great News about a month when I met Papa Herring. When I did meet him, it was hard to believe that I had never noticed him before. In the old Libby Hill turned Great News Baptist Church, with fewer than fifty members, it would seem impossible to have missed anyone. But, obviously, I had.

It was about 5:45 that Wednesday. Because I did not want to be late on my first day of Bible Study, I had intentionally given myself extra time to leave work, run by home, get my daughter situated and get to church. I was more than thirty minutes early. Believe me, that was not my normal. I was late far more than not.

My thoughts were suddenly interrupted by the sound of another vehicle entering the parking lot. Naturally, I looked up. I saw a sleek, brand-new looking, Cadillac as it wheeled in beside me. The driver's side door swung open and a tall, dark, prominent looking man stepped out. He walked to my car, keeping a respectable distance and tapped on my window. For some reason, I was not afraid to roll down my window and speak to the stranger.

"Good evening, young lady," he said as he extended his hand. "Joe Herring, here. Are you here for Bible study? You're Mrs. Thomas, aren't you? You joined our church just a few weeks ago, didn't you? You live in Sedalia and work for AT&T?"

I could only nod my head in amazement, "Yes sir." He had everything right, but who had told him all my business? I noticed it was 6:15 and still no one else had arrived. I asked Mr. Herring, "Are you the teacher and what time does class start?"

"The Reverend and a few other members will be here shortly. Probably around 6:30. We don't have to wait for them. Where is your Bible?"

We're talking the 1980s. This was before cell phones and Bible app(s), and my Bible was on the nightstand in my bedroom where I kept it.

114

Wasn't that where everybody kept their Bible? This Mr. Herring seemed to know so much about me already, I guess he already knew that I did not carry my Bible in my car. Without waiting for an answer, he instantly reached into his car, pulled out a Bible, opened it and handed it to me. Although I had not noticed it until now, he had held his own Bible in his hand the entire time we had been talking.

Then, without another word, and to my amazement, he clutched his open Bible to his heart, closed his eyes and began praying, "...Father, God Almighty, we thank you for Great News Baptist Church, for this Bible study and for all these people who have come to study your Word. Prepare our hearts and minds that we can learn the lessons that you want us to learn. Amen."

When I opened my eyes, I was shocked, again to see that several people had joined us. My car was partially surrounded by people holding hands. Someone read the scripture that I followed in the Bible Mr. Herring had handed to me. Someone else began to talk about the scripture and its relevance to what had happened in their life that day. Another shared a personal issue. Someone asked for prayer; a song was sung and someone dismissed us.

As I turned right on McConnell Road toward my home, I was in a state of awe. *What just happened!??!* I reflected on the events of that day. For starters, I recalled that Mr. Herring had never answered my question about when Bible study started and if he were the teacher. I did not get an answer that day, or the next. The answer came over the next fifteen years as a warm, caring, big brother-little sister, teacher-student relationship developed between us.

Guilt Rages On

Sister Thomas and I worked together to count the money of the church. I enjoyed listening to her wisdom; she always helped me understand the burden I carried. After one especially difficult experience, she helped me work things out with one of my daughters.

One Sunday, I gave a testimony at church. When my turn came to share, I began to speak, but slowly at first, "We are all family here at Great News. I am talking *to* my family *about* my family, and what is said in this family, stays in this family. Am I right?"

The congregation agreed and I continued. "Many of you know my story. You know that I made a choice that resulted in my incarceration. For more than half their lives, I was not there for my children. I was not there to take my son fishing, to Scout meetings, or to watch his baseball games. I did not teach my girls how to ride their bicycles, skate or do daddy/daughter things.

I know that my children were hurt and embarrassed many times when their schoolmates whispered and jeered behind their backs. It is so hard to imagine the pain they went through. I'd give anything if I could take back the hurt that I caused my family.

Thank God for my wife Dot who never lost faith in me. She stood behind me every step of the way. You have already heard how God protected and blessed me both, inside and outside of the prison walls.

What I really want to talk about this morning is something pastor and I talked about last week - guilt. Guilt is a weight around your neck that keeps your head held low. It is unforgiveness turned inward. Guilt is in your face and in your ears, whispering to you that you are nobody;

you have no worth; nobody needs you; nobody loves you; and, that you have no authority.
I wish it were easy to get over guilt. I would love to tell guilt to get off my back and let me go."

A few church members nodded in agreement. "Unfortunately, it does not work that way. What happened at my house yesterday is a prime example. The wife and I were just about to sit down to the candlelight birthday dinner I had cooked for her. We were having grilled Filet Mignon, baked potatoes with sour cream and butter, and fresh green beans. I had coffee and my Grandma Herring's made-from-scratch cheese cake for dessert. Oh, and I can't leave out the hot, buttered yeast rolls that I also made from scratch. I only do those a couple times a year for special occasions or holidays.

The phone rang. Our daughter Pat had come in town for business. She was spending the night with a friend, but wanted to come by to wish her mother, Happy Birthday. "I won't have much time. I could either come late tonight, after 9:30, or early tomorrow morning, around 8:30. I want to be on the road headed back to DC before noon."

Dot was ecstatic. Seeing her baby was all that mattered. It could be for five minutes or five hours, 10 at night or 10 in the morning. That's a mother's unconditional love, she sang into the phone, "Whatever works for you is fine with us, Baby. Just come on. We're not doing anything. We'll be right here."

I thought to myself, *Really? We're not doing anything? Is that what you think of this meal I've made for you? Nothing? Well, damn! Of course, I uttered that beneath my breath.* I felt a surge of resentment, and I was mad! How could anyone, especially our own child, be so thoughtless! She was probably in town all day. Why was she just getting around to calling her mother? Secondly, the friend she was with is probably her boyfriend. Does she really think we are too stupid to figure that out?

"Why would she come at 8:30 in the morning to make us late for church? Why doesn't she come to church with us so we can have dinner as a family afterward? That shows no respect for our plans. As a matter of fact, that is blatant disrespect! But I guess you are ok with that," I snapped unfairly at Dot.

I wanted to say to her, exactly what any Christian father would have said to his daughter two decades ago. "If you're shacking with this nigger before you marry him, why would he want to marry you? You are giving him everything he wants for free. Where is your self-respect? We didn't raise you like that."

Guilt spoke up: "What do you mean "we", Joe? You didn't raise her at all, Joe. You were in prison, remember?"

I thought about things I would say to my daughter instead, "As good as your mother has been to you, how you could make her the last thing on your to-do list? And you know that we go to church on Sunday. But not speaking what I was feeling did nothing to quell the rising tide of rage within me.

That's when I left my body. I could sense my blood pressure rising with anxiety as my lips quivered, my hands trembled, and my palms began to sweat. Fear gripped me by the throat and choked me while guilt pressed down hard on my shoulders and paralyzed me. The war within me raged on.

Guilt spoke again: "Joe, you have no right to judge her. You cannot impose your values on her. You have forfeited your rights to parent and besides, she doesn't respect you or love you. Let it go, Joe. Why don't you go shoot a few rounds of pool? Staying here will only make you mad and make you say things you will regret."

You got that right, I thought to myself as I grabbed my black leather jacket from my closet and headed toward the garage. Dot and I met in the hallway. Her eyes were brimming with tears. "Joe, where are you going?"

After a long silence, followed by an intentionally loud exhale, I slapped the car keys down on the credenza by the back door. "Nowhere."

The Anointing spoke next: "Joseph, I am your strength. Depend on me. When life gets crazy and nothing makes sense to you, call on me. You can't fix this, Joseph. Give it to me, and I will be your strength."

The expression on Dot's face spoke volumes. There was no judgement, or condemnation, just understanding, compassion and love. "I love you both so much. Why don't we just face what you're feeling? We can work through it,"

> *"I held the long-stemmed match toward the candle's wick. ...And the light came on!"*

Getting up from the sofa, Dot took the box of matches from the mantle over the fireplace, gently, slid her hand inside mine and led me to the dining room. "I am starving."

I held the long-stemmed match toward the candle's wick "And *then the light came on!*" I blessed the food, " Thank you God for Your forgiveness and for Dot's patience. Thank You for taking away my guilt and for saving a very special time which I was about to wreck. Thank You God for helping me understand that love and respect are not things to be demanded but earned."

***

We had finished the dishes, gotten into our night clothes, and moved back into the living room to take a final glance at our Sunday school lesson. When the phone rang again I answered. "Hey, Daddy, I'll be there in fifteen minutes. Can you open the garage for me? I can never get that blooming thing to lift up."

I beamed. In my heart I prayed, "God, thank You for your grace. My daughter needs me, and I need for her to need me." I smiled into the phone, "And you never will have enough strength to lift that heavy door, but don't worry. Your Daddy will open it for you honey."

"What are you smiling about?" Dot asked. "I don't know what that girl would do if she did not have me to lift that garage door for her."

"I think she will cross that bridge when she gets to it -- if she ever does."

The minute she bounced out of her car up the three steps through the mud-room and into the kitchen, the environment changed. That spirit of negativity, the venomous, hateful thoughts and words I had been spewing dissipated in a second when she arrived. When our daughter entered the house, a sweet spirit came with her.

The air felt lighter and it seemed easier to breathe. The mantle that had been pressing down on me all evening was lifted. I felt like singing a song about being able to fly and touch the sky.

Our daughter floated across the room into her mother's arms. "Happy Birthday, Mom," she held her in a long, tight embrace. She kissed her mother's forehead and pressed their cheeks together. "You are looking good, girl. Keep doing what you're doing." She touched her hair, "Is Miss Burnette still doing your hair every two weeks? Look at those sassy red nails. Dot Herring, you are saying something!"

She turned to me, "And look at you, Sir!" She glided gracefully into my arms, laid her head against my chest and pressed hard for a long time. I felt her warm tears through my shirt, and I heard her voice tremor. I held her tighter and kept quiet.

"Thank you, Daddy, for coming back to us. I know it was not easy for you. You did not know what to expect from us any more than we knew what to expect from you. We were afraid that you would not like us and that you would try to change us. Thank you for letting us be who we are. I love you so much."

"I love you too," I said through my tears. I motioned to Dot, "Come on over here, Miss Dot. Let's make this a group hug."

After we embraced, Pat said, "Let me give you your birthday gifts. I've really got to get out of here soon."

I was surprised, "Gifts? You already sent me something for my birthday."

"Daddy, this is special. She reached into her large, leather purse. Opening a small, white jewelry box, she took out a 14- karat gold tennis bracelet and fastened it on her mother's wrist. "Enjoy it!" She slid a handsome mahogany colored genuine leather wristband across my arm. "Man, this is nice!"

"It should be. I stood and watched a native tribesman make it when I was in Ghana. Look inside. It has your initials, JDH." She gave us warm hugs and kisses as she started for the garage. Then she stopped. "Mom, Dad, I don't think I will try to make it to church tomorrow. I honestly did not bring anything to wear except these jeans and another sweat shirt like this one. I would love to get an early start back to D.C. We are looking at about six hours of driving, you know."

That could have been the end to a beautiful visit, but something inside me would not let me keep my mouth closed. "Have you been to church this year, Pat? I hope God doesn't bless you as sparingly as you serve Him. With a final hug and not much conversation, I opened the door to let her out of the garage.

***

As I was telling my testimony to the church, I heard the church door open and to my surprise, a figure slipped inside, unnoticed, and sat on the back row. I recognized my

122

daughter immediately. "Baby come down here to the front." At first, she did not move, did not even look at me. But I could not let it go. I kept talking, embarrassing her, saying that God did not care about her dress. By now, of course, the entire church had turned to look at her.

After I refused to stop, she rose from her seat in total humiliation and started slowly down the aisle toward the front of the church. As she got close to the center where I was standing with outstretched arms, she sped up her steps, veered sharply to the left almost running, went around the pulpit and out the side door.

There was a loud gasp across the church! The swinging door that connected the sanctuary to the back rooms swung lazily on their rusty hinges a time or two before stopping. With nobody breathing, you could have heard a pin drop. The heavy exit door opened and quickly closed. The deadbolt lock clanged noisily, deliberately and with finality separating those inside from those outside of the church.

More gasps punctuated with "Awws" and "Oh, no's!" Anguish glazed my face. My eyes widened, my lips trembled and my heart throbbed as I slumped forward. "God, please just let my children stand and acknowledge Your Name! That's all I ask!"

God spoke to me in that moment, "There will be times in your life, Joseph, when what feels right, will be all wrong. There will be times when what you deem as wrong will be right. Let Me be the Judge. Sometimes rights and wrongs will blend and look the same. You, My son, may not know the difference."

Although Sister Irene was more like a daughter, she had a great understanding of people. She was helpful to me that Sunday. She stood up and spoke, "I know how much you want to be a part of your children's lives, but you can't force it, Papa. Allow God to let it happen. Trust me, your daughters love you as much as you love them. We have to give the relationship time to heal."

After all these years I had finally learned when to shut up and listen. I kept my mouth closed and absorbed what Irene was saying. "Papa, I learned quickly that you are a man firmly committed to what you believe. No one can talk with you for long without learning what you value. Almost immediately after your extended hand and your trademark introduction, 'Joe Herring, here,' you are quick to articulate what means the most to you. God and church are first, followed by family and home. Not supporting your church financially and not taking care of your family are cardinal sins in your eyes."

"Sister Irene you sure do know me!"

"You are big on honesty and fair treatment; hard work; cleanliness and beauty; respect, gratitude and obedience from children and grandchildren. Papa, you are a strong defender of your own truths. On the other hand, when you see that you are wrong you have one of your "And *then the light came on* moments."

I spoke up finally, "Those are my reminders from The Anointing."

"Yes sir," she said, "Papa, you are big enough to say, 'I'm sorry, I was wrong.' Go get your daughter."

I slowly breathed without speaking. I decided to let God lead me this time.

> *"Oh, the depth of …the wisdom and knowledge of God! How unsearchable are His judgements and unfathomable His ways! For who has known the mind of the Lord, or who became His counselor? For from Him and through Him and to Him, are all things. To Him be the Glory forever. Amen."*
> *Romans 11: 33,34, 36.*

File Cabinet Fallout

Brother Sherlock Bynum came to Great News first as an employee and then as a faithful member. It was later that he became our pastor. The small, intimate congregation had an amazing work ethic. We held full-time jobs plus managed our homes, families and church responsibilities. What impressed him the most was the dedication we had to getting our young church off the ground.

Everybody, including the children were eager to work. We all brought something unique to the table. My keen business sense and organizational skills made me the unofficial and undisputed Church Business Administrator, clerk and Chief Financial Officer. Honestly, I thought I was doing a fine job wearing all these hats. Only problem was that in the world of the IRS, non-profits, corporations and banking institutions our way was not legal and could have landed the whole church body in jail. Picture that!

Brother Bynum was asked to tidy up the church's records and its processes. When we were interviewing him for the position, everyone made several things perfectly clear: "Papa Herring's integrity is beyond reproach. He is totally sold-out to the good of this church."

One of the deacons boasted, "His word is his bond. If Deacon Herring tells you he is going to do something, consider it done."

Another Deacon said, "He's got a business head on his shoulders. He can tell you when, where, and why every penny was spent. Bottom line is that he has got a system that is not broke; yet, folks holding the purse strings say we've got to fix it. So, your job Sir Sherlock pun intended is to transition as quietly and as seamlessly as possible from his system to yours. Can you do that?"

"I can do that."

125

"Oh, and did I mention that Deacon Herring is territorial and a bit strong-willed?" Well, I never would have said that about myself.

Brother Bynum scheduled our first meeting on a Monday evening. That gave him time to leave his day job at Kroger where he managed purchasing for three area stores. He had a degree in Finance and Business Management from the university plus nearly ten years of work experience.

The two of us entered the church parking lot at the same time, got out of our cars and walked toward the front door. In my classic tradition I looked him squarely in the eyes, gripped his hand firmly and said, "Joe Herring, here. You must be Brother Bynum." I could tell he was hesitant. No one could be naïve enough to think I would be overjoyed about his coming in to improve the system which I had spent years perfecting. I mean, my system had been working for a while.

"Yessir, I am." He extended his hand to shake mine. Continuing my in-charge stance, I unlocked the door and invited him to follow me. "You drink coffee? I'll make us a pot if you want."

"Yessir. That would be great."

I could see Brother Bynum's mind working. I could hear him thinking, "This brother is sharp! That must be a $1,500 suit and $500 shoes. He is tall, muscular and walks with an air of authority. I guess that's why everyone loves him. He is a different kind of man."

He interrupted my thoughts when he spoke, "I can tell immediately that you are an icon, a true pillar of the church. They love and rely heavily on your wisdom." The Holy Spirit showed me in that moment that this meeting would be much more about establishing a working relationship and far less about crunching numbers.

"I love and support this church Brother Bynum. I will do whatever God wants me to do to help it succeed."

"Deacon Herring, if you will open our meeting with a word of prayer we'll get started promptly at 6:30. We should be out of here before 9." I did not think, however that ending on the same page would be an all-night process.

We took off our suit coats, loosed our ties, rolled up our shirt sleeves and went to work at the big wooden desk. My obsession with detail and process almost to a fault made me a natural for this kind of work we were doing.

When it came to me dealing with other folks' money, I had a philosophy that said "before I take it away, I'll add more to it. I don't want one penny that does not belong to me!" I was a leader and not a follower in the area of tithing and generous giving. I didn't tell young families what to do, I showed them by example.

I gave $500 per month for tithes to the church. I had an annual income of $60,000 and I never thought twice about honoring God with my money. No Colored person that I knew of, including professors at the University made that much money in the sixties. God allowed me to use my gifts to serve Him and make money for my family. That was a blessing.

About an hour into our meeting we had downed a pot of coffee and were drenched with sweat. Four hours later, we were starving and dog tired but still working. Neither of us wanted to quit. There must have been more than five thousand meticulously organized and itemized receipts stapled together. In a different stack were legal documents from the bank and independent contractors. Yet another stack held cancelled checks that had been returned by the bank and reconciled in the stack of six-inch thick account bank ledgers.

A member who worked with IBM had donated two computers: one for the Pastor and one for the church office. Brother Bynum sighed, "If nothing else comes out of tonight's meeting, we are in agreement that the new computers will replace this manual labor and paper files."

All ten tons of the papers and boxes would have to be transferred from paper to electronic documents. For that, we would need to bring in a professional data entry person, somebody who had the training. He made a suggestion, "Papa Herring, I am going to ask if there is anyone in the congregation who knows data entry. If not, then we'll hire a couple of ladies through a Temp Agency to put it into the computer. Then we can get rid of all this stuff."

No response. Brother Bynum was totally unprepared for what happened next. He was picking up the stacks of paper and trying as carefully as possible to put them back into their original boxes.

I swung the door open and it closed behind my back. "Hold on, Papa. Where are you going? We can't leave this stuff all over the place like this!" I heard him talking to himself, "Wow! And I thought the past five hours had gone well. Shows what I know. What upset him? Did I say the wrong thing? Did I make him mad?"

Brother Bynum had not annoyed, disappointed or angered me. He told me later that when I left the room he began to pick up handfuls of papers and cram them into boxes. "At this point I did not care how they went in. All I cared about was getting them off the desk so that I could go home. If you could have a nasty, childish attitude, so could I!" Now that was funny to me.

I swung the church's front door with the loudest, awfullest noise. "Brother Bynum. Brother Bynum can you give me a hand out here?" I was out of breath.

"What a relief to hear your voice but what the devil are you doing to cause all that racket!"

He locked the hinges to hold open the double doors. Then came around to the back of the huge, refrigerator sized box that I was trying to lift. It was heavy as all get out. The box towered above my six foot frame. It took us fifteen minutes of backbreaking work to get the box balanced onto the dolly and maneuvered across the threshold into the church.

"Mind if I ask what's in this box and where we are taking it Papa Herring?"

"Man, can't you read? It's a file cabinet. We got to have somewhere to put all those papers." He looked at the box as I described what was inside, "she's a 'beaut', six feet tall, ten metal drawers housed in a solid oak cabinet. Just wait until we get it opened you can see for yourself."

"So," Brother Bynum asked, "Deacon Herring, when was this purchase discussed and who authorized it?" He told me later how he thought everything we had done went right over my head.

"I authorized it myself. It was seven hundred bucks out of my pocket. Ya'll can reimburse me." I pulled a folded piece of paper from my shirt pocket, "Take the receipt. I got it at Office Furniture Depot."

"Papa Herring, I'm afraid this here file cabinet is an unauthorized purchase."

"Don't worry about it Brother Bynum."

"Well at least all that racket you were making wasn't what I feared. Do you know that I crawled beneath the desk? My heart pounded like crazy as the sound of metal like a hundred trash cans bashing against the front door shook the building. I served in Desert Storm, so I knew exactly what was going on. It was a cannon, a bomb, a missile. Maybe all three!"

I couldn't hold back my laugh. "What are you saying Brother Bynum?"

"I did not know what else to do, so I hit the floor and covered my head with my arms. Hey, don't judge me. I wasn't taking any chances with my life. What would you have done?"

I was laughing so hard that tears were rolling from my eyes. Brother Bynum was laughing too, "When you called my name I brushed myself off as I pulled on my jacket to hide the split in my pants. Acting as if nothing had happened, I strode out of the office, through the sanctuary and toward the front door. Now my arm is aching from hitting the floor and the is seat ripped out of my pants."

"I like you Brother Bynum. You are a good man."

"You know Deacon Herring; I saw a side of you today that I had not imagined. I spent all my time telling you what we were going to do about the paper, and you had a plan the whole time. That huge metal file cabinet was your dated answer to new technology. We have some work to do. Let's leave this and go home to get some rest."

"We all have lessons in mercy we need to learn. No one can win every battle. Sometimes we have to let go in order to grow up Brother Bynum."

"That's true. We do Deacon Herring."

Going to Gloucester

      Building relationships with the men at Great News Church was as hard, if not harder, than beginning a new church. In both cases, spiritual and personal ideologies, differences in social, educational and financial viewpoints and differences in personalities, temperaments, gifts and abilities made for a rocky beginning. Conflict and contradiction threatened the little church daily.

      Throughout the controversy, however, Walt; James; Phillip, Jim; Robert; Gary: George: Sherlock; Harold; Leon and others weathered the storm. They were all willing to be broken, mended and molded for God's purposes. That's when and where I came in. I knew that God wanted me to work with the young men. They were my "boys."

      I joined Great News because I saw the potential for greatness and at the same time, the potential for disaster. I could see what the inexperienced members were doing right, but I could point out what they were doing wrong. I leaned on them heavily, often using harsh and judgmental words. I did not hesitate to let them know that I "didn't take no junk" from anybody.

White churches divide all the time. On any given Sunday, you could ride through the city and find a dozen or more groups of White and Asian worshipers in downtown storefronts; in industry buildings, and in vacated credit unions, theaters and schools. As far as I could tell, these planted, spinoff or satellite churches, as they were called, were thriving. They were not considered to be an enemy or a threat to their parent churches.

From what I could see, the "parent" church provided structural guidance, wisdom, spiritual advice and financial support. Ironically, this same action in a Black church would create quite a stir, starting with a glaring newspaper headline. Words like split, rift, divided, disagreements and in-fighting were used. Individuals involved in the move were described as troublemakers, haters, or disgruntled members who, when they couldn't have their way, "took their marbles and their tithes and went home."

I felt compelled to share my personal experiences with the boys. I wanted to show them what it looked like to support, love and trust one another. They needed to encourage and respect each other. I stressed the idea "Before you can be leaders in the church, you needed to be leaders in your homes."

That is how I came up with the idea of planning individual getaways with each one. I could tell by the way they treated their wives and children that some of these boys had grown up without fathers in their lives. They needed financial planning and organizational skills.

***

132

I decided to call Rev. Lacewell up one morning to invite him to Gloucester, "Joe Herring, here," I said when Reverend Lacewell answered his phone.

"Oh, how're you doing, Papa Herring? You feelin' okay today?"

"Sure, I'm fine but that's not the question. The question is, how are you feeling? Don't you have a long weekend coming up? You get off at 2:30 on Thursday and don't go back until 6:30 Monday morning, right?"

"Wow, Papa, you know my schedule better than I do. So what's on your mind?"

"Well, I was watching while you were preaching Sunday. You seem tired. It has been in my spirit to take you on a quick getaway trip. Didn't you tell me that you like deep-sea fishing?"

"Uh huh."

"You remember my brother, Wray and his wife, Sadie, don't you? They came to church with us last year for Family and Friends Day."

"Yes Papa I remember."

"Wray has been on my back to bring a couple of you boys from church to Gloucester for some good fishing in the Chesapeake Bay. If you are at my house by 4 o'clock on Thursday, we can be on the road by 4:30 and in Gloucester before dark. It's only a four-hour drive."

I had everything planned, "We'll get up Friday morning. Sadie will fix us a good breakfast, then Wray, you and I will go fishing. The boats go out early. By 11:30 or noon, we'll be ready to head back to Greensboro."

I did most of the talking, sometimes not even giving the Reverend time to respond. "We can pay them down at the dock to clean our fish and pack them on ice for us. All we'll have to do is put the coolers in the car and head out. Does your wife know how to cook fresh fish?"

"Yes sir."

"You know there is a special skill to cooking them. Maybe we will have the whole church come to my house for a fish fry. I'll do the cooking. I don't mind."

"Ok, Papa. That sounds great. I will see you Thursday at 4."

***

Just before four o'clock Thursday afternoon, Rev Lacewell was standing at my front door with his camouflage duffel bag in hand. That was one thing I liked about the Reverend; you could always count on him to be on time.

Dot and I met him at the door. I waved my hands in a sweeping motion, telling him to back his car back to the street. I pulled my car out of the garage and told the Reverend to pull into my spot. "Just be sure that you leave Dot enough room to get out for work in the morning. I would hate for her to side swipe you." I gave her a playful squeeze around her tiny waist. "Ain't that right, Honey?"

She greeted the Reverend and handed me two lunch bags. "I know Sadie is going to have a big layout ready when you get there, but that will be at least nine o'clock tonight, so I made these for you to eat on the way." She turned to me, "Joe, doesn't digest fast food that well."

"That was very sweet of you." Looking into both bags I did a quick assessment, then handed one to the Reverend. Dot had packed two bologna sandwiches with cheese, lettuce, tomato and mayonnaise; an orange, a banana, a slice of homemade sweet potato pie, and some shelled peanuts. There was a candy bar, plus a Tupperware bowl of potato salad and a plastic spoon.

"Do both of our bags have the same things in them Papa Herring?"

"Of course not. My wife is never going to make your lunch as good as she makes mine." Yanking playfully on my lunch bag, he tried to see what was inside.

"Get away from here, boy," I said flexing my muscles and dazzling him with a little fancy footwork. "I may be twenty-five years your senior, son, but I can still put your lights out! You heard Muhammad Ali talking about the butterfly. You can't hit what you can't see!"

"Stop it, Joe," Dot said. "Somebody is going to fall and get hurt."

"Mother Dot, tell your husband that we both have the same thing in our bags."
With a sly smile and a wink to me, Dot answered him, "More or less." He was never going to win with us, so he just quit.

"Eat that potato salad, Reverend. You know, you can't play around with anything with mayonnaise in it once you take it out of the fridge, eat that first."

I shook my head at Dot. She was always thinking about things like that. I turned to Reverend Lacewell, "Send us up one for traveling mercy, will you Rev?"

I took a minute with Dot before bounding down the steps to the car. Traffic was not bad, the snacks were delicious, and gospel music on the radio kept us laughing and praising for the entire trip. I broke the ice by asking, "So what's your favorite fruit Reverend?"

"Umm. . ." Rev hesitated a long time before he answered. "For starters, what kind of question is that? And what are you going to do to my answer? This is a trick question, if I ever heard one." Rev shook his head, gave a low, throaty laugh and then said slowly, "cantaloupe"

"Cantaloupe!? Naw, you don't want to be no cantaloupe. They are mushy, too soft and too sweet for your blood. They are not solid. Don't ever tell anybody you want to be a cantaloupe."

"Well, I never said I wanted to *be* a cantaloupe. You asked what my favorite fruit was. That's different from saying that I want to *be* one."

"I'm telling you, that's not what you want to be. Don't ever tell anybody that you want to be a cantaloupe."

Reverend Lacewell spent the trip determining what kind of fruit he should be and eating the snacks Dot had packed for us. I enjoyed the gospel music on the radio and the gorgeous Virginia landscape which set the mood for God to do something great.

God, Please Hold Back the Rain

We pulled into the circular driveway that surrounded my brother and sister-in-law's beautiful, farmhouse. Flood lights came on and, in a flash, Wray, was looking and acting amazingly like a mini-me outside, waving a big flash light and telling us where and how to park. Inside the spacious kitchen, Sadie had set a table "fit for a king." By the time we finished stuffing ourselves with fried fish, creamed potatoes, collard greens, corn pudding and cornbread, we could hardly move.

While we were still sitting around the table the phone rang. Sadie answered it and handed it to Wray. "Really? Naw, I had not heard anything about rain. Where did you hear that?" He was silent as he listened to the other line, "Well, my brother and his pastor just came in from Greensboro. How much help do you have? Okay, that's eight. We might be able to make that work. Let me talk to my brother and get right back with you."

I exchanged looks with Wray and we both looked at Reverend Lacewell. I guess he had the feeling that something was up. That ominous phone call had come from Wray's neighbor, Mr. Jack Charley. This semi, well-to-do White family owned practically the entire county of Gloucester, and in their minds, that was a given. Nobody or nothing would ever change that.

Needless to say, the Charleys had not been happy campers when they learned, some thirty years ago, that two Colored Herring boys from nearby Bladen County had been combing around in the courthouse looking for land deals. Then, much to the chagrin of the Charleys, them, two Colored Boys found a loophole in a piece of land without a deed and bought it.

That was not the biggest bombshell to the Charleys! That came later when it was revealed that Wray's 28-acre plot was strategically situated in the middle of their 300 acres of lush, green, rolling farmland. To increase its value, Wray's land had a gravel surfaced easement giving him easy access to the main highway. To a passerby, it was impossible to tell where Charley property ended, and Herring property began. God does have a sense of humor, doesn't He?

A lot of stuff went down before the older generation of Charleys died and the land passed down to the younger ones like Jack. Through the years, some of the hostility and resentment faded, but every now and again, a vestige would rear its ugly head.

Agricultural work was backbreaking, demoralizing, often unprofitable and always unrelenting. On the other hand, it was addictive. More farmers than not, loved the land that they called "God's great earth." They loved their crops in years of plenty and hated them in years of failure. Among farmers, there was something bigger than life about the cycle of planting and praying for the elements to cooperate, then reaping the harvest.

The Herrings were among the handful of Negro families to own land in the 50s and 60s. It always came at a high cost: strife, fighting and sometimes, even killings. Every generation of Herrings, starting with my Grandpa, Handsome Herring. I noticed the spelling was changed from Handsome to Hanson later in his life. He was serious about two things. The first was land ownership and the second was education.

Reverend Lacewell couldn't help but notice the warm relationship between us as we reminisced fondly about our father's words, "They'll be making cars and clothes forever. You will always be able to buy that, but they ain't making no more land. Buy that whenever you get the chance."

Ray heeded Pa's advice and as soon as he completed a successful tour in the U.S. Navy, playing in the band, his heart turned to the two things he loved, teaching and farming. There is nothing more rewarding than absolutely loving the way you live.

For more than thirty years, Wray taught band at Huntington High School over in Hampton, Virginia. Every Negro kid in the Tidewater knew Mr. Herring and he knew them too. He took his students to band competitions and concerts up and down the eastern shore. Next to teaching was farming. He loved the land because it allowed him to express himself like nothing else did.

***

The next morning, I climbed out of the big, old fashioned, four-poster bed where I had slept like a log, between flannel sheets. I followed my nose to the dining room where, once again, Sadie had put her foot in it. The table was set with hot buttered biscuits with homemade jelly, country bacon and sausage, fried fish, grits, eggs and fried potatoes. To drink, we could have hot coffee, orange juice, a glass of buttermilk or sweet milk.

I ate without Reverend Lacewell who was still sleeping when I got up. Wray waited until he was finishing up breakfast before sticking his head inside the door and asking, "Come on out, Reverend. We're waiting on you. Did you get enough to eat?"

He smacked his lips, "Yessir!"

As Reverend Lacewell stepped outside into the warm, morning sun, I was standing there with Wray, a 50-ish looking white farmer, whom I took to be Mr. Charley; a lean and sturdy looking tan colored Native American with straight, jet black hair that hung to his shoulders; a short, muscular Mexican with a yellowish complexion and wavy, brown hair and two lanky, young White boys.

Although the sun was shining brightly, there were rumbles of thunder and a slight breeze indicating that rain was on the way. I moved closer to Reverend Lacewell and said, "We're going to have to change our plans because the weather man is calling for gale force winds and heavy rains to move in by daybreak tomorrow. All this hay has got to be baled up and put inside the barn. If we leave it laying out here like this and the rain comes, like they are predicting, Wray will lose everything. That would be an entire season of backbreaking work with nothing to show for it."

I explained that Mr. Charley was in the same situation as Wray, except that he had five times more grain to get up. "His giant piece of equipment rakes the straw off the ground, bundles it into a bale and ties it all in the same motion." Mr. Charley had his son and three other young bucks lined up to help him. "Mr. Charley figures that with five of them and three of us working, we can beat the rain."

Wray ended his conversation with Mr. Charley and walked over to join us. "So, ya'll want to come with me over to Jack Charley's place and help him? As soon as we are finish his, we will all come back here and work on picking up my hay."

The next eleven hours were grueling work. Mr. Charley's field was a clean as a baby's butt. Not one slither of the golden grain could be seen for miles. With five hundred and fifty bales of hay stacked snug and dry inside, Mr. Charley bolted the door on his barn with a look of smug, satisfaction on his face. Wiping sweat and dirt from his brow with his shirt sleeve, he reached inside his bib overalls and pulled out a wad of money. He counted twenty bucks into the blistered, bleeding hands of each of the laborers. "Thank you. Now git on home before these rains roll in."

He turned to his son, a husky, bronze kid in his late twenties and instructed him, "Go ahead and take the equipment to the shed. Let your mama know that I'll be on in a few minutes."

My brother's eyes and nostrils flared! You could see him bristle as he jerked his body straight up and spun around to look Mr. Charley dead in his eyes. "What the hell are you doing, Jack Charley! We are just going to leave my hay out here to get drenched? You said if we helped you with yours, you and your boys would help me."

"Oh, Wray, you will be okay until tomorrow, he said with a typical White, know-everything air of authority. I don't think the rain will come in before tomorrow night and besides, even if it does, you don't have that much hay to worry about."

Whoa! That was the wrong thing to say! My brother Wray lunged forward with his eyes fixed on a 3-foot iron pipe lying on the ground. I saw what he was thinking, and in a flash, I lunged, too — kicking the pipe out of his reach before turning to Jack Charley and snarling, "What the hell did you just say, Man?"

Fire leaped from Wray's eyes! "You low-down, dirty son-of-a-gun! Funny, you believed the weather forecast when your grain was in jeopardy. Now that mine is in danger, all of a sudden, you don't believe it's going to rain. Well, first of all, you ain't God and you don't control the rain. The weather man says that heavy rain is starting before day in the morning and continuing all through the weekend. Regardless of what you believe about the rain, we are going to protect my crop the same way we protected yours. I expect you to be a man of your word. And what the hell has the amount got to do with anything? You think just because I don't have as much hay as you do, it's okay for mine to get wet!"

Wray was fuming, "I promise you, Jack Charley, that when the first raindrop falls on this land, my hay is going to be safe and dry inside my barn. Same as yours!

141

Now, you can keep your word and help me like you promised or I've got something for your white ass!"

With those words, Wray spun around sharply on his heels and headed for his pickup truck. Reaching across the backseat and into the cab he pulled out his double barrel shot gun. He cocked his gun and aimed it straight at Mr. Charley. I lunged toward my brother. As huge beads of sweat popped out onto my forehead and my voice quivered, I pleaded, "Wray, please, please let him go! We can do this. We don't need his help. Let him go."

Wray never flinched. He never batted an eye and never turned his head. In a stern voice that did not quiver he ordered, "Get back out of my way, Joe. I know what I'm doing." Sweat was now rolling down my face as if somebody had drenched me with a tub of water. The Rev and I knew that Wray was as serious as a heart attack, so we did as we were ordered.

In the split second that it took for Wray to sling his gun up to his shoulder and take aim, Mr. Charley had made a beeline for his red pickup. He jumped inside, gunned the engine and floored the gas pedal. The truck jumped, and then shot twenty yards down the gravel road as if it had been shot from a cannon. Mr. Charley fought to control his truck as it dovetailed from one side of the gravel road to the other and nearly hit the ditch. Blasts from Wray's shotgun had old Jack and his truck dancing!

Buck shots hit the ground on either side of the truck. It kicked up a cloud of white sand and gravel so thick that you could no longer see the truck or the road. When Wray figured he had given Mr. Charley enough of a scare, he put his gun back into the gun rack, cleared his throat of all the dust, wiped his sweaty palms on his overalls and motioned with his head for me and Reverend Lacewell to get into the truck.

When we climbed inside, he sighed, "I've never seen anything like this. I don't know what got into that cracker. We've been farming side by side for nearly twenty years and I've never had anything like this happen. The low-down, double-crossing, scum-butt just couldn't stand to see me with a good harvest. Never mind that he gets a good crop every year and that it is five times bigger than mine. He is entitled to that. I can have bad luck every season, then finally I have a great crop and he can't handle it. He has to find a way to sabotage it!"

With a sigh of exasperation, "I'll never understand White folks. I am sorry, Bro. I am sorry, Reverend. I invited you guys up here to have a nice time fishing. I had no idea it was going to turn out like this. I sure didn't bring you here to run your blood pressure up, seeing something crazy like this."

After all that had gone down Wray broke down. He banged both fists against the steering wheel, dropped his head and began to sob like a baby. "I am sorry, Joe. I am sorry Reverend. Just give me a moment to get myself together. I'll figure out something. I don't know what to do right now, just give me a moment."

I moved closer to my brother and cradled his head against my chest. "I know exactly what we are going to do. We are going to bale this hay up — every single straw and we will get it done before it gets wet. That's a promise from God. Don't worry about it, Bro. We are in this together and ain't nobody going nowhere until every slither of straw is safe and dry." I turned to my Pastor, "Rev, you got another prayer in you?"

"You betcha! Ain't one drop of rain going to fall before we are done." We bowed our heads and he prayed, "Father, we thank you for this challenge you have set before us. We don't understand it and we don't know how to fix it. All we can see to do right now is to start raking straw. Thank you for working through this situation. Give strength to our bodies that we may be physically able to do this work. But most of all, thank you for holding back the rain. Amen."

Near midnight we had been working about four hours. Sadie drove up on the small tractor. "Here" she said handing us some cups, "you guys need to take a break and have something to eat."

Wray, still emotional, gave his wife a tight hug, a quick kiss and then started to protest about not having time to stop.

Ignoring his protests, Sadie proceeded to pour a hot cup of coffee and give a sandwich to her husband. "Come on, Joe. Come on, Reverend. Take care of your bodies. This ain't the first time the Herring family has seen trouble and it never stopped us before. We have got plenty of time. It's not going to rain until we are finished. I already know that. Enjoy the ham sandwiches and hot coffee I fixed."

Sadie was right. After the break everybody felt better. We were able to forget about our scratchy throats, nostrils and eyes; our bleeding, blistering hands and our sore, aching muscles. After about twenty minutes we pulled on our gloves, grabbed our rakes and pitchforks and started back to work. A few minutes later we noticed great music coming from the tiny, maroon colored, battery radio perched on top of the truck. It was tuned to a great Black station out of Nashville, Tennessee that played a mixture of Blues and Gospel.

As if good food and good music weren't enough, we looked around to find that Sadie had covered her hair with a scarf, put on her work gloves and boots, grabbed a rake, and was now raking hay like the rest of us. What a beautiful sight to see a Black woman working alongside her man through thick and thin!

Normally the Virginia sky would glisten with bright stars. That night the stars were hidden behind black clouds. As we worked tune to the radio. The previous sense of annoyance, disappointment and urgency dissolved into

144

peace. Way in the distance, the mighty waves of the Atlantic hit the shores in and out in perfect harmony. With every ebb and flow came the calm reassurance that God's universe is forever and so are His grace and mercies.

Life has its craziness, but it does not last forever. We heard the loud clanging of the hay baler. Jack Charley, with a shit-eating grin on his face joined us with a lame excuse about having had to drive fifty miles to Richmond to find a screw to replace one that had fallen off the equipment earlier. Wray did not even respond. With a solemn face, he simply pointed to the row we were on and the direction we needed to go in order to finish the job. For another hour, you could hear the clamor of the baler, an occasional rustle of an animal in the nearby pastures, a car whizzing down the road or of a train in the distance. Otherwise, we worked in silence.

Just before 2 a.m., the silence was broken by a loud, "Hallelujah, thank you, God!" Now it was Wray's turn to celebrate. He beckoned for the four of us to come and see the 100 bales of hay stacked neatly inside his barn bone dry! He threw up his hands and did a shout for joy as he clanged shut the bolt on his barn.

Wray stood still and then his body started to tremor and tears rolled down his face. We all rushed to his side to join him in what we knew were tears of triumph. As the five of us stood together, we heard a gush of wind, felt leaves swirling around us and then torrents of rain fell from the sky! In fewer than sixty seconds, we were drenched to the bone!

Except for Wray and Mr. Charley, the rest of us made mad dashes for the house. The two of them stood still as rain poured down on them. Neither man moved until an earth-shattering lightning bolt sliced right between their faces. Scrambling for safety, they grabbed each other, and then in voices barely above a whisper, we heard Jack Charley say, "I am sorry. Will you forgive me Wray?"

"I am sorry, too."

Reverend Lacewell must have waited a moment to see that all hearts and minds were clear, then standing in the drenching rain, he looked up toward heaven and exclaimed to the top of his voice, "Thank You, God. Thank You for forgiveness, for friends and for faith. But most of all, Thank You for holding back the rain!"

LESSONS IN MERCY

PART IV: LESSONS IN MERCY

Being a Father

I was released on parole in December of 1968 and what an exciting time that was for my family! While the girls were already in college, Joey was a high school senior in the throes of looking for a college to attend. He was eager to combine a career in medicine with his love for the game of basketball.

All three of our kids had strong personalities and were unusually brilliant. They had tenacity and went for what they wanted in life. I give Dot most of the credit for these achievements. She was responsible for them financially and emotionally while I was away. She got love and support from our friends and family, but that was not the same as having me there.

If it were not for Dot's encouragement, the kids would not be where they are today. Dot raised three beautiful kids singlehandedly. We would spend hours talking about some of the crap that had gone on in my absence. It was hard to believe some of the things she had gone through.

Dot told me how one of the white women she cleaned for wanted to purchase groceries instead of paying her in cash as they agreed. "I didn't want her groceries. I wanted her to pay me my money so I could take care of my children. I knew what they needed more than she did."

Looking the lady straight in the eye, Dot said, "No thank you. If you will just give me my money, I will buy my own groceries for my children. Otherwise, I'll have to find another job."

"Obviously, that lady did not know my wife very well." I reassured her.

"The following week, she tried the same trick again. What made me so mad was that she was only paying me $4 a week to clean that ten room house and she didn't even want to give me that. The next week, I was about half way finished with my work when she yelled up the steps and said to me, 'Dorothy, I have to run and get my kids from school. You can lock the back door and leave when you finish. I left your money here on the kitchen table.'"

"What did you do Dot?"

"As soon as I heard her car leave, I went downstairs to see what she had left on the table. Just as I expected, she had left one pound package of ground beef that was spoiled. Beside that was stale bread, a tomato and $1.50 which was not even half of what she owed me! I was furious! I stormed out of her house leaving her food and her money there on the table. I took the city bus downtown to The Department of Social Services, swallowed my pride and applied for Welfare."

"I never knew that."

"By the time I received the first Welfare check about two months later I had found another domestic job that paid double the money for half the work I was getting at the first job. I was collecting rent from the rental houses and the $40 from welfare made everything doable for us."

Dot did not miss one mortgage payment and I don't think the kids ever lacked anything. She made sure to be there at every waking moment. And if that wasn't good enough, she was able to manage her time and money to go back to A&T to finish her accounting degree.

Our children excelled throughout their time in school. They participated in sports, drama, and debate clubs along with being in the school choir and playing in the Marching Band. Our goal was to show them true love and forgiveness. We tried to create a sense of normalcy while I was away. Returning home was exciting, but it meant that I would have to work hard to get to know my children again. Thankfully Dot and Sister Irene were there to help me understand how to navigate through my personal guilt.

My Man Child Joey

They say you can't miss what you've never had. I disagree. My relationship with my Pa as a child did not make me feel loved and included. Even as a man I longed to get his approval. It was important to give everything I had to my son Joey. I struggled to regain a connection with him and my girls after returning home. Joey had been "the man of the house," and was no longer my little boy.

As a little kid, Joey was like me. He was inquisitive and outspoken and had a deep need to be fully engaged with whatever was going on. When I left him he was only seven years old and was faced with the same searing questions I had felt at his age. Not one day or night went by for nearly ten years that I did not pray, "God, please give me one more chance to look my son in the eye and say, "Son, I'll be at your game."

During the early days of my sentence when I believed that I would be spending "the rest of my natural life in jail" I still a glimmer of hope. When I began to find favor among the Bureau of Corrections Board and see my sentence commuted three times the glimmer turned to a flame. God was faithful during my time away from my family. He honored all the promises He had made to me on the day of my birth. I was reminded of Jeremiah 29:11 and I held on to Joshua 1:7-8.

I was angry at myself for making a choice that took me out of Joey's life during his most formative years. I know this is not how God had it planned; it was because I did not listen to the Anointing. I could have changed the script if I had not been caught in my own thoughts. I did not know how to recoup the lost years of his life and forge a meaningful father-son relationship.

The Holy Spirit has shown me mercy all my life. I would pray for direction in my relationship with my son. I prayed but didn't always take action. To say, "Okay God, I am giving this to You," and I kept taking it back from Him. That was counterproductive.

Joey's grades were good, and he worked hard. He applied to a number of Historically Black Colleges and Universities (HBCUs) and to some predominantly White schools. Acceptance letters and scholarship offers poured in from several different schools, but we were most excited when we received the letter inviting Joey to prestigious Springfield College. They were offering him a full academic scholarship, plus a spot on the basketball team in Springfield, MA.

Joey was walking on air; he could see his dreams coming true. He made plans to study pre-med and follow his sister's footsteps to Meharry Medical School. He thought about going to the NBA! Dot and I loved watching his enthusiasm. I knew he would succeed. Joey was "made for college" and "college was made" for Joey. He was a popular kid who engaged himself fully in campus activities including recruitment of minority students from high schools surrounding Springfield College.

For three years our immediate and extended family members drove ten hours and fifteen minutes from Greensboro to Springfield to watch Joey play basketball. In at least two of those years, we drove through ice and snow. One year Lizzie Ruth who was living in Connecticut with her daughter, Donna drove over to meet us.

It was a miracle that after nearly twenty years, I was finally able to answer, "Sure, Son. We'll be at your game!" I was proud of my son. He would call home to tell us about all the things he was doing around Springfield and on the campus. He was becoming a great leader and a man that people loved to be around.

The first time we made the trip, Lynda and her husband went. Another time, Wray, Sadie and their daughter, Joanie were our travel gang. For the third year, Dot and I were joined by Pat, her "sister-friend" and one of my brothers that we picked up in D.C. The road trips to Massachusetts were wonderful. Who knew a family could have so much fun together, eat so much and laugh so hard!

Our daughters had already finished college and were supportive. They encouraged Joey, sent him money, and teased him about not bringing home a White girlfriend. He sent us newspaper clippings that made Dot beam with joy. This one is a little faded but it tells about how Joey speaking to potential students about Black student life.

Springfield College **Student**

VOLUME LXIX, ISSUE 1   SPRINGFIELD, MASS.   Wednesday, October 24, 1973

Review Board Evaluates Coed Hours Program

The Review and Acceptance Board has evaluated the proposed personal hours programs of all but one of the dorms.

The committee gave unconditional approval to Gulick's, Lakeside's and Reed's proposals. Alumni Hall's program was approved under the stipulation that representatives of the dorm submit an evaluation of the program on Nov. 16.

International Hall was given conditional approval also. The committee stated that a student guard must be on duty each night until new front doors and an outside telephone are installed.

Abbey Hall was the only dorm which did not make a presentation.

They are expected to offer a proposal to the committee next week.

All that is necessary for the programs to become reality is for the dorms to follow their own procedures in order to institute the new hours.

The dorms whose programs were approved hope to have the new policies operating by Friday evening.

The members of the Review and Acceptance Board are Meg Pearson and John Herbstrep from the Dean of Students office; Dick Stoddard, President of Lakeside Hall; Pete Sipperly of Massasoit Hall and Marylin McNulty, Hall Resident of Gulick Hall.

Student Association Headed For Deficit

The Student Association has found itself to be heading for a deficit of over $800 on this year. According to Student Government President Bruce Skilin, "If we adhere to the commitments we have made through the budget hearings we will realize and overall deficit of $800.20.

The deficit, according to Skilin, reflects a discrepancies in the collection of the Student Activity Fee, as well as in the administrations of former Student Council Presidents Steve Goldberg and Ira Colby.

"Last Spring budgets were approved, contingent on a $4 per student activity fee." Skilin explained. This was not the case. "Each student was assessed only $35. The result is that the Student Association has come up $3,000.00 short of its projected income," Skilin continued.

During his administration, Goldberg called for an all campus Day of Concern. The cost of this event was in excess of $30,000.00, an expenditure which totally exhausted the reserve account of Student Council.

Under the administration of Colby, the 1973 yearbook editor, further complicated matters by overspending his budget by $18,000.00.

Due to these events neither of the administrations were able to pay completely for its yearbook. As a result, the present Student Government is confronted with the tasks of paying the balance of the 1970 and 1971 Massasoits as well as making a down payment on the 1972 yearbook.

In an effort to avoid making the forecast deficit a reality Skilin explained several courses of action to be considered by Student Government at its meeting on Monday, October 25.

"We have asked WSCB to return to us $800.00 allocated to them for a power increase. This will not jeopardize their plans," Skilin explained. "If only postpones the purchase of a new transmitter until April first at which time the money will be made available to them."

from the 1972-73 Student Government budget," he said.

"In order to make up the balance of the deficit, consideration has been given to the arbitrary cutting of all conference allocations from clubs and organizations," he stated. This would raise $1250.00, and put some money into the reserve account of Student Government which should, under normal circumstances, have a balance of $10,000.00.

According to the Student Government President, another alternative would be to cut by 1/3 the complete budgets of all clubs and organizations. "This would accomplish the same as the one forecast cut," he explained, "but would put a considerably greater amount into the reserve account." Skilin was quick to point out however, that a final decision will not be made until the Student Government meeting next Monday.

Black Center Opens

Parents of Springfield College students will have an opportunity to return to the classroom as well as experience a taste of life on a college campus as the annual Fall Parents Weekend activities begin at SC on Friday.

The program is under the direction of Billie Ondriezko Newburgh, N.Y.) and Pat Schalebaum (Ridgewood, N.J.), members of the class of 1974.

"We're making every effort to afford the parents an opportunity to experience campus life," said Ondriezko. "In addition to athletic and social events, the parents will have the opportunity to meet and talk with students, faculty, and administrators throughout the weekend."

Activities will begin on Friday afternoon with parents invited to attend and participate in regularly scheduled classes at the College.

The freshman soccer team is scheduled to compete against Worcester in a 2:30 contest which will be followed by a square dance for parents and students in the Memorial Field house at 8 o'clock Friday evening.

Varsity athletic events and meetings with faculty members and administrative officers will highlight activities scheduled for Saturday.

The Varsity soccer team will meet M.I.T. in a 10 o'clock contest Saturday morning on the "Polyturf" athletic field. Central Connecticut will provide the opposition for the women's field hockey varsity squad also scheduled for 10 o'clock.

The "City Championship" will be at stake as Springfield and American International meet in a 1:30 varsity football contest, the Mayor's Trophy Game, on the "Poly-turf."

The Parents Association will hold its annual meeting following the football game Saturday afternoon, to be followed by a question and answer session with SC President Dr. Wilbert E. Locklin, administrators and faculty members.

Saturday evening activities will feature the annual Parents Weekend Banquet at which the Parents Association Achievement Awards will be presented to four outstanding seniors at the College.

Parents Weekend Ahead

Sunday, October 13th was the opening of the Black Cultural Center, located on the corner of Manhattan St. and Walnut St. Set up by a group of Black Springfield College students, the Center has an office for director Charlie Miller, a conference room, lounge and large meeting room.

Numerous events have been planned which the students feel will make people aware of the Black culture, help the black person pride in himself and unify the cause of the Black people.

This Saturday, the 23rd, the Center will host minority group high school students from the area. Groups from the Upward Bound program at UMass and S.A.S.S.I. Prep will also be present.

A recreation program for 8-12 year olds in the community has been planned and will be headed by Keith Tilghman. Along with this plans are also being made for a tutorial program in elementary school, high schools and colleges of the Springfield area. This is headed by Richard Griffin.

A big weekend for the center will be Nov. 11, 12, 18. In addition to an open house on Sat. 13 and a dance the same night, some of the events of the YMCA Weekend will be held there. The Student Affairs Commission of the Board of Trustees will also meet at the Center.

Members of the Center would also like to sponsor Thanksgiving and Christmas parties for the children in the Springfield community.

The Black Cultural Center is open on weekdays 2 p.m.-11 p.m. and 2 p.m.-1 a.m. on weekends.

College Night For Minority Students

A college night for minority students has been planned by four departments at Springfield College. The joint venture of the Admissions Office, Black Cultural Center, Community Relations Office and Athletic Department will be held October 30 in the Black Cultural Center.

This will be one of the first events held in the center, at the corner of Walnut and Manhattan Streets.

The program is for high school seniors from Technical, Commerce, Classical and Cathedral High Schools, and will also include students referred to the college from the local community agencies and college placement agencies.

Charles Miller, staff coordinator of the Center, and program chairman Lloyd Rougier, a SC student have put together a program that will show the students a view of campus life at Springfield.

They will hear of the Black student life from Joe Herring, of the athletic picture from assistant football coach Graham Foster, of the admissions process from Ernest Jones, of the admissions office staff.

There will also be a chance for discussion groups, with professors answering queries.

Andrews New "Y" Program Director

Bob Andrews has been appointed Administrative Director of YMCA Programs at Springfield College. Andrews, of 181 Magnolia Terrace has been acting director for a year, replacing Edward Sandow, now the associate general executive of the Metropolitan Springfield YMCA.

Andrews had been the assistant director of the YMCA Programs office since 1967. He is responsible for maintaining the contacts between the college and YMCA movement, nationally, regionally, and locally. He will also be working closely with the admissions office

at the college in the recruitment of young men and women interested in YMCA work, and with the placement office in regards to jobs for graduates in YMCA work.

Andrews is a graduate of Upsala College, with a degree in psychology, and holds a masters degree in education from Springfield. He is president of the regional chapter of the Association of Professional Directors, and is on the National Recruiting Workshop Planning Committee and the National Council of YMCA's Personnel and Management Service Committee.

The Massasoit Yearbook is now taking applications for the position of Editor for the 1974 yearbook. The person will be selected by the present Co-Editors solely on the applicant's qualifications and desire to obtain the position. Contact Glen Lyons - P. O. Box 1421.

Joey Swings the Justice Pendulum

The sit-ins of the Civil Rights Movement started around 1967. Student activism was big in Massachusetts and across the country. Black students were protesting, skipping classes, and some were going to jail. Student protests and arrests were rampant throughout the country. We weren't surprised when we got the first notice about Joey's alleged involvement.

We had no reason to believe that our son would ever miss an opportunity to stand up for a good cause. I wonder where he got that from. As the protests became more frequent and in some cases, ugly; Dot and I did become concerned. We began to see on television that colleges and universities were expelling a lot of students for participating in the movement, Dot really began to worry but, she stayed calm.

That's more than I can say for myself. After the phone call saying that Joey had been kicked out of school and that he would not graduate, I went ballistic! "I don't believe this boy. He has lost his ever-loving mind." All within one week, Joey made headlines for being the high scorer in a game against the school's arch rival. He made *Who's Who Among College Students,* was inducted into a Greek honor society, took part in a protest rally, got thrown into jail and kicked out of school!

Dot and I were devastated that Joey was expelled. She was quiet about the whole mess but accepted it. Pat and Lynda seemed to understand their brother's position. Why was I the only one in the family mad?

For a couple weeks, we did not hear from Joey. Someone who said he was an Advocate representing the Black students called us, "The students are being charged with criminal trespassing and with inciting a riot."

Our first response was to get into our car and drive to Massachusetts immediately, but we were advised otherwise. Instead, we contacted my former lawyers, Lee and Stanback. They contacted the advocates and negotiated through them.

A decision was reached and Attorney Lee called us into his office to discuss it. "Criminal charges had been dropped against the four dozen mostly black protestors. The Springfield students will be suspended for one semester."

Dot and I both reacted at the same time, jumping to our feet. "Hold on, Joe. Hold on, Dorothy," Attorney Lee said, calmly. "That's not all. The provost is recommending that the kids lose credit for the current semester; but that they be allowed to apply for re-admission in the fall with a signed agreement to never participate in future protests."

Once again, Dot and I reacted vehemently. Drumming his thick fingers against the top of his oak desk, Attorney Lee said, "I hear you, but before we go any further, there is something else you should know." He took a deep breath, "Joey has flat out rejected all of this. He is quoted in a local Springfield newspaper telling school officials to 'take your proposal and your degree and SHOVE IT because I will never give up my right to stand up for what I believe!'"

Dot and I were speechless! Attorney Lee did not tell us what to think. He sat quietly and gave us time to digest what we were hearing. After what seemed like a long time, he said to us, "There is another option. The NAACP has a paralegal out there advocating for the students. He has an idea for Joey and two other seniors who are in good standing, academically to keep their credits and graduate on time. Like I said, this guy is a paralegal. He doesn't have the legal teeth to keep those White folks from railroading your son. If you want me to, I can fly up Monday morning, put some legal fire to this guy's plan and see what happens after that."

"That would be good sir." Dot was quiet.

"No problem. You know, there are some White folks and sadly, some Black ones, too who would love to see your son get kicked out of a college. In their minds, he had no business going in the first place." Dot and I looked at each other, whispered a quick prayer and then stood up to leave. I opened my wallet and took out five hundred dollars and handed them to Mr. Lee. "May we retain your services sir?"

Bringing Joey Home

On a beautiful April morning my son-in-law, Norris, my friend John and I pulled out of my driveway and headed for Massachusetts. We were going to pick-up Joey and his four-years-worth of stuff from college. Graduation and commencement activities would not take place for another three weeks but unfortunately Joey would not be present for that activity.

Before I got into the car, Dot called me back and made me promise that I would not be hard on Joey. "Hug him, congratulate him and act as if everything is fine."

To her I said, "sure, Honey." To myself I said, *"That ain't going to happen. This kid has just thrown away thousands of dollars of our money and I'm going to hug and congratulate him? Yeah, right!"*

On the return trip to North Carolina, Joey was driving and I was in the passenger seat beside him. John and Norris were dozing. This gave Joey and me some quality talking time. Remembering my promise to his mother and trying not to let my anger show, I started slowly. "Son, you know that you really didn't have the right to do that."

"Do what, Dad?" Looking, and probably thinking, just like me, my son looked straight ahead at the road and said, "It was my job. I had to take part in the protest movements. Why wouldn't I? Look what they are doing to black students. We don't get the same opportunities. How can you be mad at me, I took a stand for what I believe?" He dropped a brick when he said, "Isn't that what you've done all your life?"

"After your mother and I worked so hard and sacrificed so much, why would you think it was ok to blow it all away? Who gave you the right to decide that our

159

investment in you didn't mean anything?" I felt myself getting mad, so I backed off. If I continued, I would say something that I would regret.

There was silence for a while. Finally, Joey spoke, "Dad, I love you and Mom so much. I would never marginalize all that you are doing for me. Look at it this way: you have not wasted anything on me. Springfield has given me an excellent education and nobody can take that away from me. With or without that little piece of paper, I know what I know; and, I know who I am."

Joey snapped me out of my emotions, "Look at yourself, Dad. I don't see a sheepskin hanging on your wall, but does that make you any less than the remarkable teacher, father, husband, person you are?" He paused for a long time. "All I want, Dad is to make you proud to say that I am your son. As far as having to choose between going to jail for my beliefs and walking across a stage to receive a diploma, there is no contest! I would do it all over again if I had to."

I did not answer Joey because I was choking back tears. His timing was impeccable. Just as Dot's words, ". . . hug him and congratulate him," popped into my head, my backseat passengers came alive.

I heard John yawning. "Hey man, we need a stretch break and some food."

When we slid out of the car, I gave Joey a hug, congratulated him and added, "I'm proud of you, Son." He looked squarely into my eyes and breathed a sigh of relief.

"Dad, not all kids have parents like you and Mom who will see that they get what they deserve in life. Those are the ones I am standing for."

Thanks to God, good legal counsel and knowing good people, Joey received an Express Mail package from the postman three days after the graduation ceremonies. The box contained his gold honor cord, degree, basketball jersey, outstanding service and excellence awards and several copies of his commencement program.

About halfway down the list of "Hs" was *Herring, Joseph Daniel, Jr. (Joey).* Three asterisks beside his name indicated that he graduated with high honors. The one-line description added that he was receiving a Bachelor of Science in Biology and that he was from North Carolina.

The program was filled with autographs from teammates, classmates and professors. "Best wishes, Joey." One message read, "Continue to stand for what you believe." Another, "You have taught me so much about life." His advisor wrote, "Joey, it has been my pleasure to serve as your advisor for the past four years. You are a great young man with a brilliant future. (P.S. Your parents must be so proud of you)."

Pat and Lynda were proud of their little brother's defiance, which in their minds, was a much bigger deal than attending graduation.

Finding Joey

Joey lived with us while he looked for work. He tried P. Lorillard, one of the biggest cigarette and tobacco companies in the area. He tried a big phone company and other local companies, but didn't get hired. It seemed odd because it was the era for Black kids with college degrees. Big companies were recruiting young Black graduates as fast as they could find them.

These young, Black professionals were a beautiful sight. They drove company cars, were assigned to special accounts, traveled for company trips, spoke the company jargon and dressed for the part. It seemed that our kids were about to arrive. I knew that my three children, along with their two spouses would be right there at the top.

Who knew how priceless the next few months with Joey would be! He and I spent hours working in the yard, tinkering around the house and playing golf. Occasionally we would dedicate an entire weekend to shop for ourselves and for Dot. It was nothing for us to return from high end stores with a half dozen suits. I would always add a great smelling fragrance for Dot. I had learned that little nicety from Mr. George. I told my son, "Perfume always makes a lady feel special. Remember that when you find your special lady."

"Yeah, Dad, I'll remember that," Joey chuckled nervously at my advice.

I am not going to lie and say that my son and I agreed on everything. We bumped heads regularly. We even found ourselves revisiting the "getting kicked out of school" controversy from time to time. No matter how often we had the conversation, Joey never backed down from his position.

"I'm sorry, Dad" he would retort, "I can never just sit by and see my people discriminated against, passed over for opportunities and falsely accused. I don't give a damn about starting a riot, or going to jail or about walking across their stage to get their stinking diploma. What I do care about, Dad, is making sure that Black people get the exact same opportunities as White people. How could you get mad at me for doing that? Isn't that what you've done all your life, Dad?"

As Joey and I continued discussions like this one, sometimes late into the night, we could disagree without being disagreeable. We could hear and respect each other's viewpoint without fear of being ostracized or rejected. In the end, our hearts and spirits married. Our father/son relationship went to a higher level of respect.

I practically idolized Jackie Robinson for his tough stance against racial discrimination yet I failed to recognize the same courage and strength in my own son. I had chosen to berate him and make him feel guilty over the loss of walking across a stage. Over time, *then the light came on* and I found humility to say to Joey, "I'm sorry for not listening to you and for not supporting your stance. More than anything, I want to say I am proud of you."

Nearly a year passed when his sister called to give Joey a hot, job lead. He followed her advice, did all the right things and in less than two weeks, moved to Charlotte, NC to begin his new job. To nobody's surprise, Joey excelled and made a great impression on his superiors. In just under two years he was promoted and transferred to the corporate office in Indiana. His sister and brother-in-law had settled there so they helped Joey move into his own apartment and get acclimated to the area.

Doing well on his job and making friends in South Bend was easy for Joey. He immediately engaged with his peers and in social and community activities. Joey had even

164

met and fallen for a beautiful young lady on the job who also happened to be from North Carolina.

***

Shortly after 8:30 one cold, December morning, Dot received a frantic call at work from Lynda. "Ma, something is wrong with Joey. He was taken to Indiana General Hospital." I rushed home when she called me. By the time I walked in, Lynda was on the phone again, "Dad, you need to come now. They have Joey in ICU. They are talking about a rare virus. It attacks the heart and moves fast. Daddy, hurry, I don't know what's going on. I am scared." I could tell she was about to fall apart.

"I'll be there as quick as I can. Hold on, Baby. Daddy will be there"

I called the airport and bought a ticket for Dot to get the next flight out of Greensboro. Unfortunately that wasn't going to be until eight the next night. In the meantime, my trusty friend, John and I hit I-77 North out of Charlotte and did not stop until we pulled into the hospital parking lot ten and a half hours later.

Kind staff led us to the intensive care unit where Joey looked like a little kid lying between white sheets in that big bed. He never opened his eyes and never acknowledged us. Lynda who had been bending over her little brother, squeezing his hand and kissing his forehead stood up abruptly, ran into my arms and collapsed.

A nurse came to help with Lynda while I stood frozen, looking at my son's ashen face. My mind went back forty-seven years to the "white lady who moments earlier had been a Black lady" hovering over my mother's body in that little house on Benbow Road.

Another nurse came brought us hot coffee. "Do you want to purchase food? We did not. Then, in a very kind voice, she explained, "The doctor will come to talk with you when the rest of your family arrives. I believe he would prefer to speak with all of you at the same time."

A short time later, we were all sitting in chairs around Joey's bed. I don't think any of us heard anything the doctor said until he mentioned something about signing to donate Joey's organs! That's when reality knocked us to the ground; then picked us up and slammed us down again! "What are you talking about, Man?" I shrieked, whispered, yelled and groaned all at the same time! "What are you telling us? That Joey is not going to be ok?"

He waited patiently as some of us calmed down. "Take your time." We had to strain to understand the mid-Eastern accent of the fortyish doctor from the Middle East. "Thank God. This infection is extremely rare. This swift-moving virus looks like nothing more than a common cold but goes straight to the heart and completely shuts it down within 24 to 48 hours. The victims are usually males in their early 20s who are vibrant, active and in good health.

And just when I thought the rest of my life would be smooth sailing, this knocked me down. We were all in a state of shock. Eventually, my son-in-law, the attorney was able to translate what the doctor was asking. "Do you want to donate some of Joey's organs?" Dot and I signed the form to donate his organs.

***

The trip home to Greensboro was a blur. I don't even know who drove. I only know that it took an eternity. Joey's body did not arrive in Greensboro for eight days. Those were probably the hardest days of my life. We met with Brown's Funeral Services and to make final arrangements. We made phone calls and mailed notices to family, friends, co-workers and ex-classmates. After that was done we all found places in the house and special ways to deal with our grief.

166

I would drive for hours; or sit with Dot and try to comfort her. Sometimes I would find a vacant place in the house and allow the pain to have its way! Between crushing emotional blows I begged God to let me die. I had no will to survive. For hours on end I would vacillate between different phases of grief:

- Guilt — God is punishing me for all of my sins, anger, bitterness and wrong deeds.
- Self-loathing —I was sulking and drowning in sorrow, hating myself.
- Death Wish — "God, let me die instead."
- Punishment — "God you are punishing me for busting up another father and his son."
- Hopelessness — "What can I do?"

These feelings burdened me but I knew they would not last forever. The God we serve is not vindictive. He is a God of mercy.

The Lesson in the Loss

Wailing aloud, on the day of his homegoing I fell to my knees when the limousine from Brown's Funeral Home pulled up at the house. We were waiting to be loaded into the family car and driven first, to the church and then to Maplewood Cemetery where my son's body would be laid to rest. I beat my fists against the cushions on the sofa. Someone told me later that I had passed out several times in my living room where the family was gathered. My emotions were overwhelming.

Somebody also told me that it had taken more than an hour, several squirts of ammonia smelling salt and a change of shirts before the funeral directors were able to pull my family together and start the procession. My heart was pounding. A mixture of sweat and tears dripped from my face on to my white shirt. Everything around me was foggy. It was December 1975.

My mind raced backward to another December morning seven years earlier. In December 1968 and I had just been released from prison. Such irony! That day in December my brother, Richard and Dot drove to Raleigh to pick me up in Richard's sleek, midnight blue Cadillac and took me home to Greensboro. I felt free and forgiven. I felt like a man standing on top of the world with a brand new beginning and with everything to live for!

In December 1975, I felt the opposite after losing my son. I felt weak, dizzy and sick to my stomach. Every part of my body ached and I wanted to vomit much like I felt every time I passed Brown's Funeral Home. I felt hopeless and helpless as if God were playing, yet another cruel trick on me!

I remember the voice of the Holy Spirit on the day of my birth. I know that He told me at that time, "Things will get crazy and you will not understand where I am going with your life." I know the Holy spirit told me to lean on Him but losing my son was not part of my plan.

Joey's death almost wiped me out, but not before I learned a lesson. The agony was unbearable. But ***then, the light came on***. Joey had been young, healthy, good-looking and a brilliant twenty-three-year-old. He had a bright future. He had everything to live for and no reason to die.

The God we serve is not that kind of God. He is a God of mercy. Joey's death was not a punishment. It was the full manifestation for God's plan in my life. I clung closely to God's Word for comfort, patience and understanding. Ironically, a few days later my family had to lay my niece Joanie to rest. Wray's daughter was about the same age as my son Joey. In the midst of my anguish, I remembered that the Holy Spirit had promised to be with me; He had kept his promise even in my storm.

LESSONS IN MERCY

PART V: MY FINALE

Letting "Miss Dot" Have Her Say

Joe allowed me to tell my version of our first meeting. Now he is allowing me to share my version of our parting. This won't be easy but here you go:

In his last days Joe got to a place where he didn't want to see anyone. It wasn't that he was feeling sick, it was just that he didn't want his friends and church members to see him in what he thought was helpless or incapacitated. I always knew what a big difference Joe made in my life, but I had no idea how many other lives he had touched. Wow! It was quite humbling.

It was hard on him that we had lost Joey. He just always felt so badly about not meeting his own high standards of fatherhood. While he swore that he didn't care what people thought about him, I know for a fact that Joe did care about certain things. Our children, especially. He could be so sensitive about them.

Joe longed for the connection with Joey, Pat and Lynda that he had lost while he was away. I know he loved them, and they loved him, but distance can have a way of driving a wedge into relationships. Joe knew that.

As I watched him decline, it caused me to think about our life together. He says I was strong for him and our children, but he had a strength I could never explain.

Outwardly, Joe gave the appearance of having it all. Actually, that was not the case. Joe struggled with a serious inferiority complex, which I believe stemmed from his birth and subsequent adoption. That was hard for him all his life.

Joe and his siblings would occasionally speculate about whether Pa had contacted Mama Sallie and asked for her help with his children. They don't know if she had simply come to visit, felt compassion for Pa, and offered to help by taking the baby.

As wonderful as Mama Sallie was, Joe was never able to wrap his head around the idea that his Pa determined that he could afford six kids, but not seven. He used to say, "Why did the ax fall on me? Why was I the game changer?" Making it even more confusing to Joe's childhood mind, his dad married two more times and had three more children after him.

Mama Sallie was truly an angel. She was one of the sweetest and most caring people you could ever meet. All the Herrings loved her. I still don't know if there was a blood relationship between the two families. What I know is that, in Joe's mind, if he had to be adopted, there was no better person to do it than Mama Sallie Carroll. They had an amazing mother/son relationship that endured every hardship they experienced.

We all need to learn to find goodness, mercy, and laughter in every situation. Don't waste time thinking about what happened in the past or what will happen tomorrow. Just live in the moment. Joe had a hard time with that. I used to say to my children all the time: "Don't let your mistakes define you. When you make one use the "4 L" theory:

- LOOK — look it squarely in the face, acknowledge it. Say aloud, "I did this. Be specific. Name the sin."
- LEARN — analyze it but not for long. Learn from it.
- LAUGH — It is not always possible but try hard. This can put you in touch with your humanness and ease your burden of guilt.
- LET IT GO! — this is the most difficult but essential step in the process.

From the day we met in the auditorium of my high school, I saw that he was never without a plan. Never during our forty plus years together was there a time when his mind was not racing and planning ahead. I would often say to him, "Let's just take a break, Honey. We haven't finished X or Y yet and you are already racing ahead to Z." But that was not his style. Joe loved and lived by the scripture, Proverbs 20:5:

> *"A plan in the heart of a man is like deep water, but a man of understanding draws it out."*

When Joe began to decline in health, church members would call and ask how he was feeling. I know this was their way of finding out if we were home. A short time later I would hear a car in the driveway. I would invite them into the house and go into the bedroom and say to him, "Honey, the pastor and a couple deacons are here to see you. Although it required extra energy and extra oxygen from the tank he was using, he mustered enough strength to protest, "Tell them I'm resting. They can come back later."

When Pastor Bynum could hear him protesting, he would say, "No problem, Papa, we'll pray where we are." Pastor Bynum would pray in the den with everybody encircling me. At other times, despite Joe's protests, he would say, "Come on ya'll, we want to lay hands on Papa." Then we would all move into the bedroom.

Joe would keep his eyes closed tightly and his lips pursed closely to make us think he was asleep. None of us believed him; however. We knew that Joe was being Joe. "Didn't I tell you that I did not want to be bothered, today?"

"Yeah, you did, Papa, but, today, we chose not to listen to you because we love you so much."

They would devote the rest of their visit to making me feel better. As we sat around drinking tea or coffee, whichever they preferred, everybody had a funny story to tell on Joe. I still laugh when I think about some of the things that we shared about Joe during those last few months of his life.

I know Joe would say those were some of the most cherished moments of his life when he could look back and see his life in review. On good days when his breathing was easier, he would hear the stories folks were telling about him he would join in the conversation, laughing and disputing their versions of what had happened.

At other times, he would not talk. He would look at the person talking and then at the rest of us and shake his head. We would all get a good laugh and the person talking would continue talking as if to say, "It's my story and I'm sticking to it."

During his final seven or eight months, beginning late summer of 1994, Joe's strength and energy declined rapidly. What he hated most about that was that he wasn't able to go to church. "His boys" as he called them, came and picked him up and took him to church around Thanksgiving and maybe one other time. He grew so weak that they decided to not try it again. They continued to bring Communion and visit him.

Although he wasn't in pain it was a struggle for Joe to get out of bed. People were aware of his condition, so they never came more than two or three at a time and never stayed more than thirty minutes to an hour.

Everyone wanted to take shifts sitting with Joe. Although their kindness was overwhelming, I never took them up on that offer. I always wanted to be the one with him if he ran into difficulty during the night.

Everybody just loved Joe. People showed so much love, respect, trust and forgiveness for Joe that I must admit that I sometimes felt a tinge of jealousy. They came from all over.

During Joe's illness and ensuing death, hundreds of people came to me with essentially the same message about him being a remarkable man, a man of God's own heart."

Joe was never too ashamed or too proud to talk about his life. He could look squarely in your face and talk about his wins, losses, failures and successes. Joe made his mistakes, like all of us, but what I liked about him was that he never tried to place blame on someone else; he always took full responsibility for whatever he said or did.

Joe was a good man. He was a man who showed us what God's mercy looked like in person.

The Life of
Joseph Daniel Herring, Sr.

April 7, 1928 - January 5, 1995

It is Thursday, January 5, 1995. I will not live to see my sixty-seventh birthday three months and two days away. Inside the sprawling, recently renovated Moses H. Cone Hospital in Greensboro, my life is about to end. Just as He was with me in my beginning, the Anointing is with me now.

As I mentioned earlier, human minds are not supposed to be able to relay the details of our births and deaths. This goes beyond the realm of natural and into the spiritual. As I lie here, in sweet repose, on this cold, crisp and sunny, January day, I feel a smile creep stealthily across my lips.

Those lessons in mercy when I said, "***Then the light came on,***" have shaped me. I thank Him for the times He held back the rain in my life. I hope you will learn your lessons in mercy too.

Right now, I feel him beckoning me to trust Him again. I sigh in release. There is a faint smile, a final squeeze of Dorothy's hand…nobody else can hear it, but God softly declared in my ear, "You have completed your assignment."

Joseph Daniel Herring, Sr., son of the late Eugenia and Hanson Herring was born in Guilford County, Greensboro, NC on April 7, 1928. He was guided by a devoted and loving adopted mother, Mrs. Sallie Carroll. Mr. Herring retired from Cone Mills Corporation. In later years, he was self-employed.

He joined Great News Baptist Church under the leadership of the Reverend James Lacewell and served as a Deacon and the Father of the Church for nearly ten years.

Survivors include wife, Mrs. Dorothy Melvin Herring of the home; daughters, Dr. Patricia Herring Jackson (Julius) of Okemos, MI and Mrs. Lynda Herring Wilkerson (Norris) of Indianapolis, IN.; sisters, Mrs. Mildred H. Thompson of Area, HI, Mrs. Sadie Anders of Garland, NC; brothers, Wray R. Herring (Sadie) of Gloucester, VA., Richard L. Herring (Barbara) of Greensboro, Jefferson D. Herring (Essie) of Chattanooga, TN.; five grandchildren, Rahsaan, Sajida, and Ajani Jackson, and Ashley and Therese Wilkerson; and a host of nieces, nephews, and other relatives and friends.

He was preceded in death by his son, Joseph Daniel Herring, Jr.

REFERENCES

Andrews, Evan. (2104) "11 things You May
        Not Know About Jackie Robinson"
The Word for You Today Daily Devotional
        (2018) by Celebration Inc.,
        Sept/Oct/Nov edition, pg.
https://www.greensboro.com/obituaries/article_3a74e39d-
43f5-5605-
8d3f-d7d8b5dd78e0.html

APPENDIX A: BASEBALL

Joe memorized the statistics, studied the personality, and analyzed Jackie Robinson's interactions with people. He was proud of his hero that he held a degree from UCLA and wore jersey #42 for the Brooklyn Dodgers. Jackie Robinson was the first and only player to have his jersey retired across the League.

While he was impressed with his hero's accomplishments in baseball, Joe was more impressed by his stance against social injustice. It spoke volumes to him that a young, Black kid, who had so much going for himself, was unselfish and courageous enough to stand up for others.

Jackie Robinson was a flagship for breaking down racial barriers. Born with an acute awareness of injustice he was never afraid to speak out. A man of superior intelligence, self-discipline and courage with a passion for equality, Robinson had everything it took to be an agent for social change in areas including politics, military, entertainment and business.

In the summer of 1949, Robinson was called to speak before the House on Un-American Activities Committee. The request came in the wake of a controversy surrounding the black singer and actor Paul Robeson. Robeson had remarked that African Americans would be unlikely to support a war against the Soviet Union after receiving such dismal treatment at home. Asked to comment on black loyalty to the American way of life, Robinson responded with a speech denouncing communism and the evils of racism.

While serving in the U.S. Army, Robinson experienced discrimination in the way Negro soldiers were allowed to apply for the *Officers' Training Corps*. He was infuriated as he watched White soldiers, were far less

183

qualified than some Negro soldiers, rise through the ranks while Negroes with superior skill and intellect remained at the bottom. He sought the counsel of his friend (and fellow soldier) Joe (*The Brown Bomber*) Louis. Over a few rounds of golf, and some late-night strategizing sessions, the men began an immediate protest. They refused to back down until the process was changed. The result was a breakdown of many racial barriers. By the time Robinson left the military, he had risen to the rank of 2nd lieutenant, and saw other deserving Negro soldiers promoted as well.

After retiring from baseball in 1957, Robinson devoted himself to the civil rights movement and to the plight of American Negroes. After several non-productive meetings with President John F. Kennedy regarding race relations, neither man gave up. Eventually, they found common ground and formed a successful partnership. Jackie Robinson made history again when he joined ABC-TV Sports as the nation's first black baseball announcer. In 1965, he became the first black vice president of a major American corporation. That was something to see!

Not all White folks were racists, nor were Negroes the only ones subjected to their hatred. During one of Jackie Robinson's games as a Brooklyn Dodger his teammate, Pee Wee Reece put his arm around Jackie in a show of solidarity, and Pittsburgh Pirates player, Hank Greenberg, a Jewish ball player who had endured his own run-ins with racism offered Robinson words of encouragement. Team solidarity may have started in 1946 with Pee Wee Reece's group hug, but it did not end there. Major league athletes would continue to use their platform to speak out against injustices well into the 21st century.

APPENDIX B: REDBONES

Joe wanted to tell you so much more about Redbones and the Herring family history but there was more information than time available. As he explained to you, Mama Sallie was his first teacher. She made sure Joe understood his history and the history of people around him. Joe was known for having a story for everything. That is the teacher in him. He thanked the Holy Spirit and Mama Sallie for the gift.

Let's start with a little bit of American history that you won't find in the textbooks. The vast expanse of land between the Atlantic and Pacific Oceans was neither vacant nor setting idle, waiting to be discovered by White explorers from Europe. It was inhabited long before the arrival of explorers like Magellan, Vasco da Gama, or Christopher Columbus.

These original inhabitants of America's land from sea to shining sea included Native American Tribes like the **Lumbee, Cheraw, Cherokee, Keyauwee and Moratos** on the east coast. Native American tribes continued westward to Biloxi and Sioux Falls until they reached California.

Early and accurate history shows that these beautiful people with reddish brown skin and straight black hair populated the entire state of North Carolina where evidence of their expertise in areas, like hunting, fishing, planting and irrigation was everywhere. Their use of huge boulders and fallen trees to build dams and re-route rivers was not only ingenious but in use long before its time.

As European settlers continued to arrive in the early seventeenth century their greed was malignant. Community elders like my Grandpa Herring said their greed could never be satisfied. From their fertile rich farms in the plateaus, mountains and

> *God made us all equal.*

185

foothills of North Carolina Native Americans were driven to small towns along the coast like Elizabethtown, Whiteville, Lumberton, Ahoskie and Pembroke.

Grandpa Herring described how the greedy and power-hungry Whites ransacked and stole land and possessions from Native Americans. They stole their history, heritage, customs and culture. You won't find this in history books; according to oral history, as many as a dozen Herring men rose up in rebellion and sought retaliation against slavery and its perpetrators.

Sometime after the arrival of these European settlers, big ships filled with human cargo that looked like me pulled into the docks of Charleston and Savannah. While Grandpa Herring was not brought into this country on one of these ships, his parents were. Along with their parents and siblings they had been herded off these ships like cattle and sold to White settlers as human possessions.

His Grandpa Herring learned about the evils of human trafficking firsthand from his parents. He also witnessed inhumane treatment and blatant disrespect for Negro families by their White masters. From what I am told, it was not in the Herring DNA to watch social injustice. We did not suffer in silence, nor could we remain silent when we saw one group of people mistreating another without cause. God made us all equal.

Now to answer your question, what are Redbones? I'm glad you asked. Redbones are mixed-race babies who were born neither fully Negro, Caucasian, or Native American who resulted when despicable, old White men and boys raped beautiful, young Negro and Native American girls. These people are resilient and proud despite their difficult history!

APPENDIX C:
DESEGREGATION

On Tuesday, May 18, 1954, Supreme Court Justice Thurgood Marshall made an unprecedented ruling, "Segregation in public schools must end with all deliberate haste. Every school in the nation will have to desegregate and allow both White and Colored children to attend the same schools. No more Separate but Equal." This was the headline that blared across the front page of the Greensboro Daily News. Responses were fast but not all furious. In an unexpected response School Superintendent Ben Smith said "Our city will not delay. We will comply."

Later that week, the nine-member school board, which included my oldest brother, Elijah met to hammer out details. When the meeting ended there was a unanimous agreement that Greensboro would desegregate its public schools!

In an ironic twist of fate, what followed that decision was everything but quick and compliant. Seventeen years and three months passed before the last school would be officially desegregated! This gave our city and state the dubious distinction of being last in the nation behind Mississippi, Alabama and South Carolina to desegregate its public schools!

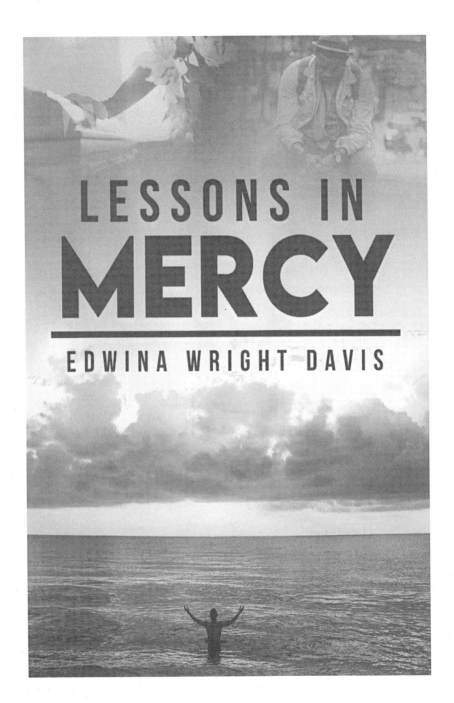

DISCUSSION QUESTIONS

1. Describe Joseph Daniel Herring's personality and temperament as he navigates various stages of his life.
   - What personality traits do you have in common with him?
   - Have you ever experienced feelings of loneliness and abandonment? How did you deal with them?
   - How did Joe manage his own feelings of loneliness and abandonment?

2. Do you know of anyone who was adopted? Can you recall any struggles this person faced with identity crisis or with socialization?

3. A recurring theme in this story is forgiveness. Give an example from the story of Joseph being the Forgiver.
   - What example can you share of him being Forgiven?
   - Share a personal example of forgiveness in your life.

4. Joseph Daniel Herring navigated life for 66 plus years; sailing was seldom smooth. The twists and turns were always tumultuous and often life-threatening. In the end, he emerged victoriously. Why do you think a smile crept across his lips at the end?

5. Do you know your God given purpose?
   - Share individuals and/or circumstances that have confirmed your Purpose.

6. On the day he was born, Joseph was given a purpose, a promise of support, and a plan/strategy for achieving success.
    - Do you think every Believer is so equipped or empowered? How are you so equipped?
    - Describe a memorable moment in Joe's life when **the light came on** for him. Why does this resonate with you?

7. How did Joseph feel about racial, social and economic injustices in our society? Look for incidents in the story where he specifically points out areas of racial discrimination.
    - How did this make Joseph feel?
    - How do you feel?

8. Only in recent decades have families (particularly families of color) begun to openly discuss adoption, infidelity, death in childbirth, incest, poverty or abuse. How did your family deal with these topics?

9. Was Joseph a product of his environment, his genes or both? How does God's mercy play a part in Joseph's personal and spiritual development?

10. What lessons have you learned from Dot about marriage and family?

11. What questions do you have about Joe that are still unanswered?

ABOUT THE AUTHOR

Edwina Wright Davis' gift for writing became apparent when at age four, she began to journal the experiences of her dolls, "This is the story of Little Sally Ann who could never stop …" She wrote about playmates and family members in storybooks and plays, "My brother's little legs pedaled as fast as they could as he rode his maroon and white bicycle into the raging rain and wind of Hurricane Hazel. He was yelling back at me, 'Get to the basement. I'm going to get Mama'."

During the years while manuscripts lay dormant in Edwina's heart or in dusty file folders, she regularly enrolled in writing workshops and classes. She read religiously and joined book clubs. For a time, she followed her writing passion in *WFMY* TV-2's news and advertising divisions. *Behind the Lines in Greensboro* also by this author, is printed by, and available through *University of North Carolina, University Press*. It is a television documentary that follows that city's long, seventeen-year trip from segregated to desegregated public schools.

Edwina's source of inspiration and encouragement comes from real life conversations with great writers whom she knew and respected including: Dr. Johnetta B. Cole; Dr. Maya Angelou; Dr. Pearl Cleage; Dr. Coretta Scott King; Actress/playwright, Ruby Dee; Dr. Daisy Daggert Buckner; First Lady Penda James; Reverend Garnett Huguley; Dr. Karla Scott; Ms. Linda Joyce; Mrs. Pamela Wimberly Jones, and Mrs. Joy Ellen Williams.

193

ACKNOWLEDGEMENTS

Dr. Patricia Herring Jackson, thank you for sharing your sensitive memories of your father.

Donna, it was an honor to hear about your special times with Uncle Joe and Aunt Dot.

Joyce Staten, thank you for sharing the powerful connection between the Herring and the Carroll families.

To Reverend Sherlock Bynum and Reverend James Lacewell, thank you for sharing treasured memories of your friend.

Phillip & Ressie Cole, your reflections have made this a most enjoyable journey.

Robert Bullard, I loved your stories of Joe digging people out of the snow.

Irene Thompson, you gave me the personal side of Joe which I tried to incorporate into the story.

George Santos, thank you for your wonderful contributions.

Thomas, thank you for using your gift of service to be my BFF, logistics manager and chauffer. Without you, this would never have been realized. You are the love of my life.

My son Tremain, you are the voice of pragmatism! "Do what works, Mom. Stop wasting time with what does not work. Buy a computer then you can talk seriously about writing your book." Always continue in this vein. It helps me. I love and respect you for being non-judgmental.

My son Trenton, you probably share my vision more than any because you are a writer with the gift of encouragement. Nothing inspires me to work on my books more than one of our long, late-night conversations. May they never stop.

My daughter Tori and son-in-law Fredrick Byrd, thank you for your sweet and loving encouragement and your acts of service. Fredrick, thank you for being such a great fact finder!

Joy Ellen Williams, Archival Historian, thank you for your love of historical research. Your help was invaluable to me.

Pamela Wimberly Jones, you have been my encourager and accountability partner for 50+ years. You helped me reach this goal. At Bennett College, you always did exactly what you were supposed to do, when you were supposed to do it. Me... not so much. I have always been inspired by your work ethic.

John Jones, thank you for being there to help in every way that I needed your assistance.

Les and Edith Millsaps, thank you for your 50+ year friendship and for always being excited about what excites me. Les, I love your illustration of Joe's car!

First Lady Penda L. James, my Scribe Coach. For the patience and dedication, you showed in getting me to the point of knowing that I am a writer gifted and appointed by God.

Check out our other titles on our website:
www.inscribedinspiration.com